A DARK ROMANCE

Cari Silverwood is an Australian author and a New York Times and USA Today bestselling writer of kinky darkness or sometimes of dark kinkiness, depending on her moods and the amount of time she's spent staring into the night.

When others are writing bad men doing bad things, you may find her writing good men who accidentally on purpose fall into the abyss and come out with their morals twisted in knots.

If you'd like to learn more or join my mailing list go to
www.carisilverwood.net
Also Facebook & Goodreads:
http://www.facebook.com/cari.silverwood
http://www.goodreads.com/author/show/4912047.Cari_S
ilverwood

You're welcome to join this group on facebook to discuss Cari Silverwood's books:
https://www.facebook.com/groups/864034900283067/

Also by Cari Silverwood

The Princess Tied

Clockwork Stalker – a romance with a cursed Sherlock Holmes as the anti-hero.

Ruled – dark scifi romance
Condemned – dark scifi romance
Mesmer – contemporary dark romance

The Machinery of Desire Series (dystopian scifi slaveworld romance)
Acquired Possession

Claimed Possession
Fated Possession – a novella
Branded Possession
Exquisite Possession

Dark Monster Fantasy
Prey
Steel
Blade

Nightmare Rising (cowritten with Nicolette Hugo)

Dark Hearts Trilogy
Wicked Ways
Wicked Weapon
Wicked Hunt
Dark Hearts trilogy collection
Wolfe – a spin-off novel from the Dark Hearts trilogy

Pierced Hearts Series
Take me, Break me
Klaus – a novella
Bind and Keep me
Make me Yours Evermore
Seize me From Darkness
Yield

Preyfinders Series (Erotic romance scifi)
Precious Sacrifice (Originally published in the anthology, Kept)
Intimidator
Defiler
Preyfinders – The Trilogy

Preyfinders Universe
Cyberella

The Badass Brats Series
The Dom with a Safeword
The Dom on the Naughty List
The Dom with the Perfect Brats
The Dom with the Clever Tongue

Squirm Files Series (romance spoofs)
Squirm – virgin captive of the billionaire biker tentacle monster
Strum – virgin captive of the billionaire demon rock star monster
The Well-hung Gun – virgin captive of the billionaire were-squid gunslinger monster
The Steamwork Chronicles Series
Iron Dominance
Lust Plague
Steel Dominance

Others
Santa with a K
31 Flavors of Kink (based on the true story of a couple exploring BDSM)
Three Days of Dominance (kinky paranormal romance)
Rough Surrender (historical romance)
Cataclysm Blues
Blood Glyphs
My Romance Curse
Fan Anonymous

Epic Fantasy
Magience
Needle Rain

Sacrificed to the Sea

CARI SILVERWOOD

Editing:
Nerine Dorman find her on Twitter @nerinedorman
Cover design: Cari Silverwood

To join my mailing list and receive notice of future releases:
http://www.carisilverwood.net/about-me.html

If you'd like to discuss this book with a group of other like-minded readers, you're welcome to join my group on facebook:
https://www.facebook.com/groups/864034900283067/

ACKNOWLEDGEMENTS

To my wonderful beta readers, Janine Peta, Emma Rose and Louise Hallet.

CHAPTER ONE

As they dropped her to the deck, lightning cracked, flashing on the maddened faces of the two men tasked with killing her. They'd flung the hatchway wide and hauled her, kicking and writhing, into a hurricane.

The sky was wilder than she'd ever seen it, and already the power and fury of the storm drenched and chilled her. Frigid water charged across the deck, dashing at her face, tugging at her dress, as if to take her prematurely.

She screamed, her throat tearing with nonsense babbles. The men turned their eyes from hers.

Swiftly, they silenced her pleas with a cloth gag.

Bound as she was, at ankles, wrists, and arms, she could do nothing as they carried her across the clipper's deck.

Beneath the roar of the wind, she was carried, beneath the towering waves trying to smash them from the rolling deck of the ship – muted, terrified, and abandoned by every other human on the vessel. She cursed them in her mind even as she feared for her life. Above, the rigging and masts lurched beneath a swirling chaos.

The rain thudded at her skin. The cloth in her mouth tasted of oil. They'd silenced her. Ashamed of what they did, perhaps. Even Guffrey, the ship's carpenter and the man she had last bedded, had turned away as she was accosted.

This storm threatened to take the ship, and she was a woman and bad luck – no matter that she'd been welcome to whore her way across to Ireland until this storm found them.

If they sacrificed her, they might be spared.

She cursed them again then sobbed and laughed all at once. Her tears were a paltry contribution considering what the sky and the sea were doing. Water washed across the timber deck as if the sea had already claimed the ship.

Grim-faced, the two men took her closer to the rail, lowered her, then steadied themselves, and made the sign of the cross on their chests. This was their last, desperate sacrifice to save a doomed ship running before the wind with bare masts and tattered rigging, with the keel likely to give if the winds and waves strengthened.

They didn't speak, though the storm would only have torn the sound from their mouths.

They picked her up between them, by legs and shoulders, and hurled her over the rail.

A mighty wave curled past and followed her down. She might drown before she reached the sea.

That would be a mercy.

There was none.

She fell – still trying to free herself, as if she could swim to safety, as if the ropes were not knotted tight and cutting her skin, as if she were not already condemned.

No one lives without hope.

She tried to free herself and failed.

The sea did not grant her the final grace of allowing her to slowly sink. It swallowed her in one ravenous gulp, gobbled her into its foaming gullet and drove her fathoms deep. In seconds she was buried under tons of water. Her hands were still bound at her back, her arms to her sides, and her ankles clamped fast and hard together, so that the bones hurt where they pressed at each other.

Her red dress wrapped her gently like a shroud.

Silence filled the void as she sank. The storm noise became distant.

The last bubbles from her lungs were lost to the roiling sea, in the bedlam of a hurricane angry enough to roll the ship a few seconds later, to pour in until its holds were bursting, and then to drive it under.

Drowning, terrified, and lost, she felt her body begin that effortless plunge. The shadow of the ship followed her down. Beneath lay a mile-deep trench. A place to sleep.

As her heart beat its last weakened *thud-thud*, something bit her at neck and back, tore away her clothes, and released her from the ropes.

But she was gone. Already, Raffaela was a limp, lifeless thing, and the surface was too distant to be reached.

Her open eyes saw nothing but cold black.

In the black, something lusted after her, something strange with sharp triangular teeth.

It feasted on her, plucked at her, thrust into her. It gave her life. A new, if transformed, *life*.

When her eyes saw again, the carpenter was falling past her, tumbling to the very bottom. Where he would hopefully rest and rot.

"Curse you, all of you," she croaked from her sea-swept, sea-scoured, salt-cured throat.

Somehow, her words reached her ears.

Her heart began to beat again and something dire swam away from her, lithely sweeping at the water with a sinuous tail.

No one came to tell her what had happened or what she

had become. She was alone beneath the waves, and although that by itself was clearly a miracle, she was unsure as to what sort of a miracle. Were there bad miracles?

The sea had become her world. She could breathe and move and swim rapidly. It came to her easily, naturally. What was she?

By feel, she found she had sharp teeth that were smaller than but similar to those she'd seen on sharks.

By sight, she found her pretty tail – a long hefty, scaled thing. The scales had a pearlescent shimmer lent to them by the light filtering down to where she swam. The tail propelled her through the water with power and grace, or so she judged it to be.

There was no one to disagree with her.

Over the weeks and days she glimpsed others like her, but they kept their distance. She did not understand or know their reasons, but it seemed wise to do the same. She was frightened of what someone like her might do to a new addition to the … species.

Was she a mermaid? It must be so.

Or was she something else, something more monstrous?

An undefined hunger dwelled inside her, and it seemed to be waiting for something.

Catching and eating fish, seaweed, and various other creatures she tried to not examine as she bit into them, calmed her, but it did not last, and always that deeper hunger waited.

Eventually the clouding of her mind drove her to swim upward, closer to the surface. Up there her new, shocking hunger might be sated. It raged at her while her body grew numb and her limbs prickled with drifting pains.

She popped her head above, into the air, and found she could still breathe, though the air lacked the clean taste of the sea. The scents of mankind pulled her to the ships that sailed by. After several days of following the ships then losing them, she ceased to deny herself. She was weaker and hungrier, yet also more able to smell *them*, their flesh, their lusts and their urges, Closer to land, where hills rimmed the horizon ahead of her, the ships often slowed. Some of them kept together like schools of fish.

Fishing boats. The men called to each other as they cast their nets.

She swam closer to a boat swaying back and forth in the waves, and there she found her first prey. A young man, merry of face, concentrating on his net while he hauled on ropes.

He saw her and frowned.

With a hold on the boat's side, she lifted herself and her breasts, above the water.

The man froze.

Then she opened her mouth and sang to him in a voice that pricked him with desire and kept him staring at her fixedly as he approached. With the slightest of tugs, she pulled him closer. When he fell over the side, she slowly lured him deeper, downward, pulling off his pants and wrapping him in legs that had newly formed just for this purpose. To spread them, to fuck a man while he drowned, to kiss him as he thrust, to take him into her world. Finally he was spent. His mouth gaped, his wide-open eyes glazed over, his chest stilled. His limbs washed to and fro like pale seaweed.

Though she had tasted his blood at his neck, it was his death she sought.

Then… his life rushed into her, a fresh and glorious sun to heat her, strengthen her heart, and give her the force to go on.

She watched as he sank.

Many hours passed before guilt assailed her. She curled into a ball, hugging her tail, unsure when it had reformed but not caring. She'd killed. A man. So she could live. It was a terrible, sinful, wrong thing she had done.

A life for a life, though, her desires told her. It wasn't so bad.

Curled up, she stayed huddled on the bottom for a full day. *Siren. That is what I must be.* Though really, she still wasn't sure.

The next morning, when the sun rippled on her skin through the water, she took a deep breath, frowning at herself and surveying her long, pretty tail, and she vowed never to do that again.

But the hunger was not to be denied. She called it the Ravening.

Judging time by the moon, she calculated that every few months she had to kill a human to survive. Sometimes it was sooner, sometimes later.

Exactly one year after she became this strange creature, at sunset, she felt the urge to swim to shore. As she reached the shallows, her legs formed, and she found she could walk and breathe as a human again. Naked, she walked onward, found a village, stole some clothes. When a woman approached her to ask who she was, she pretended she was mute, afraid that opening her mouth would reveal some monstrous part of her.

Her teeth were not sharp – she felt them with her tongue after the woman moved on.

It might have been more of a problem if what was happening did not feel so surreal. She could not stay for more than a single day.

The following day, at dusk, she went back to the sea.

The years passed, and consuming fish and men became her routine.

Her one courtesy to her past, she vowed never to forget who she once was or her name: Raffaela.

She said it to herself many times. She crept under darkened piers and clung to the barnacled posts to listen to people talk, and afterward she repeated the words to herself. When she ventured onto land, once a year, she exchanged a few words with people, if they seemed safe. Over the years the way of words changed. Language changed. Saying the new ones was fun. She must not forget how to be a human.

Raffaela.

Sometimes, she swam to a coral reef that poked above the sea at low tide. There, she sat in the air and said her name out loud to the fish that slipped by. Her voice croaked from disuse. The fish flicked their tails at her. The warm sun glittered on her naked skin and on her scales.

Raffaela.

When her throat grew raw and her skin dried, she dove back into the water and under the waves.

Many years passed. Many hundreds of years. She was alone and lonely, of course. How could she ever do anything to remedy that? Once, she'd seen a pack of her own kind, a school of them, whichever was the right word for it, tear apart a trespasser who'd swum too close, until all that was left was a slowly spreading cloud of blood.

Then one day at dusk, she swam to the top because the Ravening was upon her. Raffaela came upon a becalmed sailing vessel with a man sitting on the gunwale edge. He was talking and laughing. It was the laughing that fascinated her. With her head above water she heard him clearly. He threw his head back and the last of the sun haloed through his thick hair.

He was beautiful, the most beautiful man she had seen for all her hundreds of years, though the laugh helped too – it was so full-throated and brimming with soul.

She needed him and only him. And so she swam to him singing quietly, and he turned and found her with his eyes, though the light in the shadow of the hull was dim.

She called to him and he leaned over and slipped into the water with her. He let her drag him down many fathoms in seconds, for she used her powerful tail.

Above, someone had cried out his name, "Merrick, come back! Merrick!"

By the time her legs had formed and wrapped him to her, he was probing at her with his manhood, pushing, straining to open her, to penetrate her fully. He shoved in, lubricated by her response. This was such a thick and hard cock that she groaned and mimicked his recent movement – she flung back her head and arched, as he drove himself into her.

She saw his face in between biting at his neck. He suffered her small wounds, enthralled by their sex, pumping at her, pulling her to him with his large hands on her hips.

They fucked gloriously as she bled him, nipped him, consumed his mouth with her mouth. As he consumed her. The kiss was as addictive as the sex and their eyes stayed on each other. She could see the moment when reality dawned on him. When he knew what she did to him.

This terrible and bloody intercourse had already lasted far longer than was normal.

Somehow, she was keeping him alive, breathing her breaths into his mouth while they kissed and fucked. And then, to her dismay, she felt him lose the battle with life.

His life passed to her, and he died.

She wept as she saw the dullness come over his beautiful eyes. She cried tears of silver that floated away as she released him to the depths. The ocean swallowed him, and he drifted lower beneath her feet. With her throat locked by grief, she wept some more.

What had she done?

He was different. He could have been hers. If only she knew what to do to bring him back.

She dived with him then and tried to breath the life back into him, but to no avail.

Again, she released him and turned away, and she swam for hours, for miles. She found herself in the middle of the ocean with nowhere to go, no future, with nothing at all of worth to make her want to exist.

In the morning, still overcome, she returned to find his body, to do with it… well, she knew not what she intended but…

Something.

She could not find his corpse. This had been her hunting ground for the past half century, and she knew every cranny, every underwater cavern, yet she could not find his body.

Some predator had taken it.

Which only reinforced her uselessness.

Never before had remorse knifed into her and consumed her so mercilessly. It was as merciless as she had been to the humans she killed. That night, to consider her path from here on, she went to her coral reef and thought, while the moonlight silvered the waves.

She closed her eyes and spoke aloud to the moon and the sea. This vow she did not want to renege upon, not like the last time when she'd just begun and was a novice at killing.

"Never again will I take another human life. Never." Raffaela bit her lip with her sharp teeth. She would let herself die. It was for the best.

How to die though? Merely letting herself weaken and

expire from lack of food seemed awful. It should be quick yet not too quick. She deserved some pain.

For close to a month she dithered about, staying in her hunting area. Her time to walk upon the shore was coming. So was the Ravening but she dearly wished to walk on the land again. Could she hold off the hunger for long enough? She must choose a way to end herself. A shark would be repulsive. What else, though?

A peninsula lay beside her reef. She swam closer to the shore. There were hills here and among them she might find an unclimbable chasm. When her day of being human ended, she would surely dehydrate and die if she could not find the sea. That seemed fitting – to die near where Merrick had died, plus she would take her last breaths as a woman should, in the human world.

Except, when she swam to the beach, at the dead of night, there was a man sitting on the sand near the jetty where boats were moored. That alone would have meant little.

He saw her. He watched her swim by and followed every deviation of her course.

Something covered his face and eyes – a hunk of metal and glass such as the human divers wore. It made him resemble a monster. He saw her every move, even though the moon had not yet risen, and the night was as black as her sins.

Curious, she swam closer and into the shallows. She had no urge to kill. Yet.

She meant to die anyway, so what harm could this do, to speak to a man? He held no harpoon or weapon.

"Who are you?" She wrapped her arms about the anchor rope of a dinghy and stared across the sand. "Can you see me?"

He nodded. "I can see you."

"Oh."

This gave rise to a dilemma. She was curious about him, but the Ravening was also strengthening. He was new and different.

"I've been studying your kind. You're a siren?"

The moon was rising at his back, lighting up the sand with subtle tones.

Those few words of his had ignited her interest to heights unknown for centuries. Who was he? She must know more. And when she saw the chain that led from his leg to a vehicle parked higher up the beach… her fate was sealed. She must know more. The centuries of monotony had worn on her – of death and hunger, of an ocean full of creatures that she could not talk to.

She hungered for words.

"Perhaps I am a siren. I don't really know. But what are you?"

He dragged off the mask and his gaze wandered over her appreciatively, she thought, dwelling on her breasts. She knew how much men loved those.

"Just a man doing some research on your kind and you… A beautiful woman."

Not siren – woman.

She smiled at him, tentatively, trying not to show her teeth.

CHAPTER TWO

"Do you have a name?" He leaned forward a little too eagerly. Or was that her imagination?

A name. She knew it but gifting her name to him seemed reckless.

Still, she said it. "Raffaela, and what is yours?"

"I am known as Wolfgang. It's German, though my parents are not from there and neither am I."

He didn't smile, he merely kept watching her as if she were the most curious thing, ever.

Which she was to him, of course. When she was human, she'd read stories about sirens and mermaids and had been told of drawings too, though none of the sailors she'd spoken to had seen one.

He was studying her kind and had lain in wait for her. Had she been spotted at her coral reef? She must be more cautious.

"How did you know where to find me?"

"The news stories. Sailors tell tales about men drawn to women frolicking in the ocean. Around here, those go back to early last century. How many of those stories would be about you?"

Her?

She felt her hair lift and drop in the waves washing by. "I don't know." One hand sank into the wet sand on the bottom. The cool, shifting feel of it under her fingers reassured her.

"You are famous, or your kind are."

The instinct to not reveal herself was strong and she'd never broken this law that seemed embedded in her cells. Not until now. Only those she lured saw her up close.

What harm could it do?

He held up a small rectangular object and it flashed bright light at her. Raffaela shielded her eyes.

"What is that?" She had seen them carried about.

"A cell phone. We use it to talk to each other."

Which made no sense. She was talking to him now, without one of those. With only her eyes showing, she blew some bubbles and thought to herself. Such nonsense.

"Will you stay and talk to me for a while, Raffaela?"

An invitation. A question. How long was a while? An eternity seemed to have passed since she'd truly conversed with a man. Loneliness had whittled away at her soul. If she talked to him before she died, it would not negate the true repentance she felt for what she'd done to Merrick.

As long as she did not consume this one.

She shrank into the waves a small distance, eyeing him and the chain leading to his leg.

"Where are you going? Are you okay? Did I say something wrong?"

If she told him she could kill him when the Ravening took hold of her, he would run away. She meant to deny the hunger but if she were this close, would she be strong enough? How many days did she have? Ten? Fourteen? It was not that exact.

"I can stay and talk to you, this night."

"This night? Tonight? Good. Very good." For the first time, he smiled. "I want to learn about you and your kind. Your habits, your desires, your society… Everything you wish to tell me."

Raffaela nodded, slowly. There was something about this smile of his that was strange. As if he already hungered for her, as if she had already sung to him.

She must be careful. One night only.

"Tell me about how you call to men and pull them into the sea."

A shocking request.

The moon was behind him, placing his face in shadow and making his eyes seem black and mysterious.

She stared. He knew more than she'd thought he did. He knew she killed and had unerringly gone straight to the core of what she did not want to tell him.

"It's okay. Did I surprise you?"

She hesitated and shifted her hold on the dinghy rope. The tide was coming in, creeping up the beach and closer to him.

"See this?" He held up the leg chain. "What sirens do is a part of legend. I knew already. This is my precaution."

"Oh. I see."

He hoped that would stop her from taking him? Would it work?

It was something she'd never considered. He might chew off his leg to get to her.

"Jason and the Argonauts."

She switched her gaze to his face. "I remember that story."

"Yes. He was tied to the mast, and his men had their ears plugged with wax, so they would not be lured by the sirens." Wolfgang dropped the chain. "I should probably get my answer from the horse's… from the mermaid's mouth. Will my solution work? I said mermaid, didn't I?" He rubbed at his lightly bearded chin.

"You did, and I could be either. As for the chain…"

She remained silent as she thought. Could she know without trialing it during the Ravening? Would it stop her killing him?

This was an important point, because if it worked, might she not have someone to talk to?

As in forever?

Or until he died. She imagined herself returning week after week. He would die before she would, but it raised possibilities. And hope.

Then her fantasy was dashed by cold logic.

She had to kill men to live.

Eyes fixed on his, she decided that even if he wanted to talk to her, forever, she would be torn by guilt. She was weary of killing. Remembering what she had done to Merrick added a final stamp to her decision.

But first, his question?

Never had she considered the possibility of killing a human on land. Imagining it made her stomach churn. Blood spilled on the sand and soaking into it. The grit sticking to her. Their legs tangling as they made love. The sticky residues of human lovemaking – she recalled that too. The dirt.

So much dirt.

The sea was clean.

Raffaela lifted her head, and she looked up at the star-strewn sky.

"If it stops you coming to me, it will work. I find the idea of going to you, there, on land, horrid." She shuddered then ducked her head beneath the water to wash herself clean of the horrible thoughts.

"Okay." Wolfgang laughed. "I know the chain will hold. The shackle can only be undone with a cutting tool that I left in my car. I twist in a steel rod to fasten it and must use a hacksaw to get free." He gestured casually at the vehicle. "My car. You know of those?"

"Yes." She knew of these inventions. "I've seen them in villages and have also seen them driven over bridges that span small parts of the sea."

What if she could make him go to it and get this tool?

Hah. She shrugged. The Ravening was not sophisticated. It was a furious desire that washed her mind of most thoughts. When human, she had been able to read some letters. She didn't think any letters would make sense while the Ravening had her.

"You will be safe. As long as that does not cut straight through your leg."

Frowning, he touched his leg. "You appear eager to talk to me."

"Yes. I am. This is… new."

"And so I can trust that you have not lied to me?" His gaze was keen, predatory even – she'd seen sharks look at her like that. She eyed him back, confused. A man was not a shark. Then his mouth twitched up at one corner. "Sorry, but I had to ask."

"Oh!" Raffela giggled, something she'd definitely not done since she had died and been reborn a mermaid. "No. I do not lie." She wriggled higher up the beach, though keeping herself in the water. "You are safe now anyway. The Ravening is not upon me."

"The Ravening?" He fetched something from behind him — a squarish device like a slate, and his fingers danced upon it. "Tell me about this."

Should she?

What harm could it do? None.

"Also, you said you know of cars from seeing them on bridges? We've had them a long time. A very long time."

He waited then, and she guessed that was meant as a question.

Telling him she was centuries old seemed a key to something. Perhaps she should be frugal and not tell him everything?

She raised her right hand from the water and waved it, vaguely, scattering droplets. "I forget how old I am."

"I see. But this Ravening?"

"That is when…" She swallowed. This seemed even more terrible when she contemplated telling him. "It's when I have a need I cannot deny."

He nodded, encouraging her.

"I take men into the sea." Her words were muffled in her ears, as if another said them. "I make love to them." She'd been a whore by trade. Saying that was the least of this. "I take them far down. Fathoms down." Deep breath. "Then I drown them." And she bit them. Smelled and consumed them, bathed and breathed in their blood.

He peered at her keenly for several seconds then looked at his rectangular slate and danced his fingers. "Why? Why drown them?"

"It feeds me."

The waves sloshed back and forth several times. She wondered what he thought. That she was an abomination, perhaps. It was true. So true. And she waited for him to get angry or insult her, or to stand up and walk away.

"I see. And… how do you make love when you have a tail? If that's too intimate a question, we can skip it for the moment." A terse smile was directed her way. More finger tapping occurred.

Mouth agape, she blinked. "I change. I have no say in the change. I have legs again."

"Ahhh. Interesting! Again, though? As in… you used to have legs? What are you saying?"

"Once, I was human. I changed."

That seemed to disturb him, and he remained silent awhile.

"Will you tell me how it happened?"

The suggestion flashed her back into the hurricane, into being thrown overboard. "No." She shook her head. It was long ago and too painful a memory. "I cannot."

"I see."

He kept asking questions, and most of the time he ignored what she did and kept tapping. But he also stopped and let her ask him some questions. She told him about her place where she went, to sit on the coral, to think. About the pretty fish there, the dreadful sharks, and many other things.

This was a conversation, for sure, and she relaxed into it, rested her elbows in the sand, and found herself smiling back at him.

She was talking. To a man.

Her excitement must have showed, for he chuckled at her exuberance more than once.

Dawn approached. She eyed the paling horizon. "I must go." And she half-turned, tail swishing, alarmed at having spent so much time with him that she'd forgotten others might see her if she were here in daylight.

"Wait! Wait. Will you come back? Please?"

She looked to him, and the pleading in his voice did

something inside her… put a crack in her heart, maybe. Oh dear. He wanted to see her again? He wanted her to return. That alone was momentous, wonderful.

She noted how he'd grasped at the sand, to one side of him, like she had done. How taut were the muscles of his arm. Fine, manly muscles. Perhaps he too found comfort in the feel of sand, though the slide of fingers into wet sand and the squish of it inside her fist would be far nicer.

For a second, she imagined how his arm would feel under her hand. How he might taste.

How his blood—

She shook away that thought.

"I suppose, I could?"

"Tomorrow night?"

Her eyes stayed wide. For the first time she realized she could see his face properly – his dark wavy hair that sprang up in random curls and fell across his forehead. Large sinewy hands, which she always loved on a man. Remember though. He could never be hers. Never. It would mean his death.

She gnawed her lip gently, wary of the points.

Not hers.

She must think. "In three nights then."

"Three? Done. I will be here. You promise?"

"I said so."

"Uh-huh. You did." Slowly, he withdrew his hand from the sand, brushed it off on his pants. "Your Ravening won't come yet?"

"No." She let her teeth show, and he looked curious. "Not for a week or more."

Then she dove into the sea and did not turn back, did not look over her shoulder until she was down among the seaweed and bottom dwelling creatures, the crabs, the mollusks, and the stalking, antenna-waving lobsters. A niggling and horrid feeling arrived, a feeling familiar to her from when she was a human and mistakes had been made.

What had she done? Had she said too much? Her mouth had said too many words. She'd let him see her in her true form for *hours*.

That had been lovely. Talking, listening, and learning.

Three nights. She was returning in three nights. She must ask him more questions. She must find out who he was.

* * * * *

Three nights later, when she surfaced a little earlier in the night than the last time, he was there waiting, settled into a low chair with the leg chain leading up the beach. As she swam to the edge where she could stay submerged yet keep her head out of the water to talk, he sat forward.

"Hi! You came, Raffaela. Thank you!"

The thanking brought a warmth to her chest, right in the middle.

"Hello, Wolfgang." She blew a little spurt of sea water, feeling playful. His scent was stronger. He was a male human, of fine reproductive age. The need to touch him had strengthened.

The Ravening neared, but then it always did. Its cycle was inevitable.

"I wish to question you, Wolfgang."

"Of course. Of course." He hitched a pair of black-rimmed spectacles higher on his face. They were new. She wondered if he could see her well without those. "Your prerogative, though I hope you'll answer some of mine also."

"Tell me." Rocking up and down on the waves, she rested her chin on her upturned hands, her elbows in the sand, as before. "What are you apart from a seeker of mermaids?"

"Ha! A seeker of mermaids? I suppose you could call me that. My job?" The moon was up earlier too, and his frown lines were obvious.

"Yes. Your job." The words were rolling off her tongue ever more smoothly, the centuries of disuse falling away. "What do you do to make money?"

"I'm a marine biologist. I study everything that lives in the sea. Such as you." His mouth widened in another of his inscrutable smiles.

"Me? Hmmm. I knew that. You learn from books?"

"Do I learn from books? Yes. Sometimes. And from examining specimens in the laboratory, and live ones when at sea in boats. And from the internet."

An odd word. *Internet.* In his gaze, she recognized that curiosity as to what she knew and what she did not.

"I don't know what that is. A type of net?"

"Of course you don't. The internet helps us humans to send things around the world, without actually going there."

"Such as? Furniture? People?"

He barked a laugh. "No. Sorry. I shouldn't laugh." Wolfgang rubbed at his chin and leaned back into his chair. His slate was already on his lap. "We send words. Books, in a way. Pictures, drawings. Paintings. Moving paintings. And they get to their destination very quickly. In seconds, unless the net is crapping out."

She made an *O* with her mouth, not quite understanding. "That sounds like magic?"

"In a way, it is. But then… you are magic to me. You don't exist according to science. There are stories, myths, and legends like the Argonauts that mention sirens and mermaids, but it's considered fantasy."

Raffaela blinked at him, listening to the shush of the waves against the shore — the rolling shift of water, sand, small stones, and seashells.

What could she say to that? She whispered, "I wish…"

"What did you say?"

"Nothing."

She wished she were a fantasy, that none of this had happened to her, that she'd reached Ireland and found a husband, a good man, like this Wolfgang seemed to be. She'd had a life ahead of her, back then. It was all merely wishes, and maybe she would have died of the pox in a back alley, but she'd had hope.

Sadness swelled through her, making her want to weep. She held it in.

"So. Anyway. That is how I make money. I study. I had enough of it – the money – from my work and an inheritance, to buy a house on the shore only a few kilometers away. It's further down the peninsula." He pointed to his left.

She followed where he pointed, wondering if she could find his house. Wondering if he ever strolled the shore at night, unshackled.

The Ravening was speaking to her, hinting, insinuating.

She stared at Wolfgang. He'd been kind to her. He would never be hers. *Even if*, then she shut her eyes for desire was rising. Where her legs might be when she transformed, there, in the middle of her, she felt the stir of lust.

"Are you okay?"

"Yes." She smiled at him. "I can't talk for as long this time."

"A pity."

"The Ravening is starting to speak to me. I will get dangerous to you soon, in a few more days. In a week, definitely."

There, she'd been honest. Raffaela grimaced. Now he

would leave and never talk to her again.

"But now you're okay? I'm shackled. I am safe." He nodded firmly. "We can talk some more."

They did talk. They chatted, to her immense delight. They laughed at each other's stories – though hers she kept to ones about the ocean, or people she'd listened to from under a jetty. Things that sailors had done that she'd heard them speak of. She was cautious and did not tell him of her human past.

Something about Wolfgang nudged at her, sometimes. As if she missed some nuance, which was likely. She'd been poor as dirt and had never been a poncey sort for balls and carriages and la-de-dah. Never had enough food, most days. Learning about the changes in the way people spoke from overheard jetty conversations hadn't teached her much else. *Taught* her much else. Even thinking about her past made her speak funny.

Before the moon traversed much of the night sky, she decided to leave.

She had listened to him talk about his adventures in life and had reciprocated with her shipwreck and storm stories, and hints of what she'd found at the very bottom of the ocean. Treasures, he thought. Corpses were also a part of life down there.

"Time to leave," she said, huskily. She had worn out her throat.

"Oh." He reached behind his chair and pulled up a palm-sized, drawstring bag. "If you're leaving, I have a gift for you. A present." He raised his eyebrows. "Will you accept it?"

A gift seemed stranger than strange. Men were her prey. They did not give her things, apart from their lives.

"Perhaps?" She was curious. "Ummm." She craned forward, as if to get a better view. "What might it be?"

"Here." He tossed the bag and it landed near enough to her that she could reach it without leaving the water. Luckily. He could not have come to her, and she would never have wriggled from the sea to get it.

Cautiously, she undid the cinched neck.

"It's safe. It's a necklace. A special one."

"Safe? How would it not be safe?" Raffaela drew it forth, and found it was a string of pearls that glowed luminously under the moon. The clasp was simple, a screw-in thing. She thought she could manage it, but… wariness made her question him. "Special? How?"

"If ever you are in trouble, if you press on the large black pearl, which is actually not a real pearl. It will signal me. Then I can find you, help you."

She frowned at the weird piece of jewelry made from things she could find herself on the ocean floor, inside oysters. "How?"

"It's… like the internet. A signal goes out. Like that."

Do not look a gift horse in the mouth — a saying from her childhood.

"Thank you." She slipped it around her neck, hesitated then found the clasp, made the pieces meet.

"You just sort of screw them together." He made a circling motion with his hand. "It won't fall off once fastened."

"I have it. It is done." The pearls felt odd and heavy sitting there, above her bare breasts, where nothing usually sat.

A gift though. And one that had consideration to it. He thought he could find her in time if a whale swallowed her? Amusing man.

"Will you return again? In three days, at dusk?"

Three more days and the Ravening would be three days closer. She heaved out a sigh. "Yes. I will not stay long. I may not come if it's too dangerous."

If I want to eat you.

"Sure."

At the last second, before she swam away, she had an urge to give something to him. A piece of knowledge would be the best she could gift.

"Once a year, my body changes back into being human, and I get to walk upon the land again. For one day only. That day comes soon." She cocked her head at him, half hoping, perhaps, that he would offer something…

He looked stunned.

Stupid. She should not have said that.

She leaped and dived deep, sliding through the coolness of the sea, before he could say anything.

Stupid, stupid, stupid. He is only studying you, furthering his knowledge, nothing more.

* * * * *

THREE DAYS LATER

As soon as she surfaced, she knew. The niggling desires had been building, but seeing him before her made her throat close. She wanted to sing to him, to drag him down the beach to her.

Dangerous? Yes. She could control herself, but the risk was there.

"I cannot stay," she said loudly from further out in the small bay than before, the bottom unreachable by her tail.

For a second, he looked angry. There was light here. A lantern on a pole was shedding light on his beach.

"Wait!" He stood, shoving out his hand as if to catch her. "When do you walk on the land?"

She halted, put her hand to her heart to quieten the beats. "Why?" Then she told him anyway. She was still hoping. "In ten days' time."

"Go do what you have to do, then in ten days meet me at dusk at the beach in front of my house." He pointed. "A bay like this. Blue roof on a two-story house. A sailboat and a dinghy are moored. A long hedge with white flowers sits between house and sea. Can you find it? Raffaela?"

Her name on his lips...she swallowed. "I can. I will be there. Why, though?"

Why. The crucial question and the answer might shame her. Would he walk with her? It was meant to be her last time on this earth. Her last walk.

"Well. Because I found out a new legend, I thought..." Wolfgang adjusted his glasses. It was sweet, the way he did that. "You see, I've been reading, scouring the records, looking for something that would help." He wiped his mouth with his hand, rubbed at it again then took his hand away, shoved both hands in the pockets of his black pants. His next words came out croaky. "It is said that if a siren makes love to a man on that day, when she walks as a human, that she will never change again."

The gleam in his eyes as he said that... unmistakable.

She drew a deep shivery breath — cold wafting through her, spiking her nipples, and demolishing thought. He wanted her. And what if this tale of his was true?

"Will you be there?"

She drew a breath. "I will be there."

As she swam away, she realized what he must have known. To do this, to be there that day, she would have to satisfy the Ravening one last time. She must kill a man.

And what did she really want? If she changed and stayed a human? There was a momentous allure to that.

To be a woman again. Was it worth killing one more time so as to stop it forever?

Yes? Surely, it was a yes?

CHAPTER THREE

A few nights later, she gave in and dragged a man from a boat to his death. She swallowed his blood and his life force, then let go of his corpse to allow him to drift away on the currents. Sharks waited at the edges, cruising by in sharp gray shadows. They knew food was coming.

To meet with Wolfgang again, she'd had to do this. It was this or eat *him* instead.

Yet she grieved, covered her face with her hands and cried into the ocean.

Fuck this, as humans now said.

She had done what she must. Soon, if he were correct, this would be over.

Besides, Wolfgang must know what she was doing. He must know.

It meant he accepted murder in order to possess her.

It puzzled her.

Somehow, that had a perverted justice to it.

A life for a life, her dirty conscience piped up. Sure it was. She hated this.

The day when she walked on land arrived, and she'd been so concerned and confused, her stomach so full of butterflies, or perhaps full of a school of minnows, that she hadn't eaten anything since the man.

As soon as she surfaced, she saw Wolfgang waiting for her on the beach. He stood there unshackled, with no chain, dressed in a neat pair of dark pants and dark gray shirt, with those cute spectacles on his nose.

He stood there and trusted she had not lied to him.

Well.

Raffaela held her hand over her empty, anxious belly as she wriggled to the shallows. With her palms propped on the sand, back arched, and with kinked tail she waited for the change, felt her legs form and shudder into being, her body shifting.

Then she stood, with water dripping from her, and very aware of her nakedness.

Usually this lack of clothes was so normal, she barely realized she was missing them until she walked on a road. Then she would find clothes somewhere, somehow, pull them on, and then go to a village to gawk at the people going about their life. They'd be doing their chores… Riding bikes, talking to each other, driving cars, or looking at those glowing rectangles that Wolfgang called a cell phone. She had seen them before but had not understood their importance.

Tonight, or perhaps tomorrow, since she did not know the timing, she might stay as this. How weird it would be to be permanently human.

What if he were wrong?

That thought had been going around and around, for days.

Wolfgang approached her, walking down the slope

through the sand, shoes in one hand and with his other hand stretched toward her. "Welcome to my house, Raffaela."

She gave him her hand, unsure if that was what he wanted, and he took it in his warm fingers, brought it to his mouth…

And he kissed her hand.

Mouth open, she found herself struck again by a sense of wonder, that plummeted straight into doubt a second later.

"What if this does not—"

"Shhh." He shook his head. "No."

The transition from suicidal to wanting this… this humanity, was so great she felt sure she would explode or disintegrate on the beach as they walked hand in hand toward his house.

"That's my ocean pool." He gestured at a blue-lit square of glass, double a man's height. Water lapped at the top, forming a line. Fish swam in there, gliding by. Seaweed swayed against the light at the bottom. "The pool came with the house, but I adapted it to take full salinity sea water. Helps with my studies."

"Oh." Sand crunched underfoot, sticking to her feet. She stopped and lifted a sand-crusted foot. "Ew."

The one thing, well, one of the things she did not like about land life – things clung to you.

Wolfgang chuckled, squeezed her hand. "Come. You can wash that off, and I have a gown you can wear."

Beside the pool, a path of square, orange-brown paving stones led to the back door of the house.

She had her feet washed under a tap just before they reached the door.

Wolfgang squatted and helped to encourage the sand to wash away by tipping the water over the right places. It felt good to be cared for like this.

She bit her lower lip, surprised, as she often was on this

land day, by the lack of sharp points on her teeth.

"Thank you."

"No trouble. Such pretty feet." She blushed as he rose. He drew her to the door, opened it. "Come. I ordered takeout. It's food from a restaurant in town."

The scents were amazing, and she lifted her head to sniff. Real people food. Spices. And on plates, she supposed.

"*Mmm.* I haven't eaten for days. I was worried."

"Why?"

"Ummm." When she turned to him, she caught him looking at her nude body, his focus cruising lower to the join of her legs where the female part of her existed. As before, she'd grown a triangle of light red hair.

In his hand was a white, slithery gown he'd fetched from a table by the entrance, and also a towel.

A smile broke onto his lips. "I apologize, but you entrance me, at times." The smile was that mysterious one she'd seen before.

A second before, his expression had been different. Unused to deciphering human faces, she wasn't sure what it meant. It was not simply lust.

She must relearn this. *Body language.* If she hadn't listened to humans as avidly as she had, she would be totally lost.

"Put that on, then let's eat."

He helped her to dry herself, then to lower the gown over her head. It slipped over her body, falling into place on her breasts and other curves.

"Beautiful." Wolfgang urged her forward with his hand at the small of her back, above where her rear swelled. Funny, how that placing of his hand stirred warmth, desire.

Desire was much of the purpose of this night.

When they were seated at a table made of rich, brown timber, with chairs of what seemed to be glass, he began doling out food from several boxes of white paper. Plates, yes, those were here, and metal things to spear the food. The smell made her stomach rumble.

"I thought tonight we could have an intimate meal. The town has loads of cafés and restaurants but those we can try another day." His smile came and went. "Now, what are you worried about? I can guess."

Raffaela blinked. Sitting at a table, on a hard chair, sitting *still*, without water on her skin, it felt so very wrong. As if someone had frozen her in mud. Stifling.

His question, though.

"I am afraid this will not work."

He poured something red into a goblet. Wine, she reminded herself. Though she'd never drunk from anything so fine. The goblet was a piece of glass perfection.

"That making love to me will not cause you to become human, permanently?" He finished pouring into the glass in front of her, placed the bottle on the table.

Bluntly said. "Yes." That had reawakened her anxiety.

"Don't. What will be will be. Fate will decide this."

Truth. She inhaled deeply. "And if this fails?"

"Then you return to the sea, and we think on this some more. There might be a trick to it?"

She nodded. Would she go back to the sea? The change always gave her forewarning, and she had intended to stay here, to die. Now? It seemed ridiculous to lose all hope when Wolfgang believed in her.

"Let's eat. I'll bet you've not had wine for…" His eyebrow crooked upward. "Centuries."

She smirked. "A woman should not reveal her age."

"Ahhh." He raised his own glass that sloshed with a clear wine. "To becoming human."

She lifted hers. "To being human." Her first sip had her

grimacing. So tart a taste.

He laughed at her and picked up a knife and fork, indicated the food. "Can you use these? If not, fingers are okay. It should be cool enough."

"I think I can do this." She frowned at the hard feel of the metal as she turned a fork in her hand, then she poked her food.

The food was delicious. The wine fogged her mind somewhat, but soon after they finished eating, he led her to a bedroom. The luxuries humans possessed now, and so casually, it was stunning. No dirt, no bugs, everything clean.

Without further talking, he took the necklace from her neck and placed it aside, then drew her dress upward to her waist and pushed her to the bed. She was aware enough to know his seduction was as workmanlike as that of men who had bought her in the past. They had humped her against walls in alleys, then they went home again, or they had gone back to drinking. Pay her and move on.

This economy in his seduction surprised her but she felt too sleepy to worry. Protesting would be silly.

When he was finished, he withdrew from her, left the room, then returned a few minutes later. He switched off the miraculous light on the ceiling and lay with her in the bed.

That he didn't quite lie down was odd. The love-making had been so rough she'd hurt at times. She should talk to him.

But…

Her eyelids were heavy, her yawns frequent, and the room was gradually blurring.

This bed was terribly soft. *What if I don't feel the change?*

The worry roused her for a moment, but it was not enough to truly stir her. Sleep came with little warning.

She woke to something shifting, to her body moving, then

drifted back to sleep. Too tired. Too dark and heavy.

She woke again, and her eyes refused to focus. Had she become a sloth not a human?

The third time she surfaced, she lazed about in water, lying prone and slipping to and fro. There was a ceiling above. Something rumbled.

Raffaela shifted and found herself somehow fixed inside a tube that was open above, like a small tunnel. She had been in underwater caverns and tubes. This was not that. This was *wrong*. Alarmed, she shook her head. Water sloshed under her shoulders and something had been jammed across her mouth.

Her tail lumbered, moved, swished and smacked the sides.

Tail… She hadn't changed. She coughed and felt sludge in her throat, swallowed, blinked away the last of the stuff making her vision blur.

Where was she?

She flopped about, curving upward at the waist, finding her hands trapped behind and under her. Wriggling achieved nothing except to make this canvas tunnel sway, and she slapped her tail down, hard, in anger.

Everything lurched. The rumbled ceased. There came a great, long, echoing slam. Then a light switched on above. As she squinted upward and around her, she heard someone grunt, then a face appeared above.

Wolfgang. He grinned at her.

"Awake, are we?"

Clearly, she was not of human form.

"Wha—" She managed to say, tongue hitting metal. The rod fastened across her mouth and between her teeth made speech difficult.

"What am I doing with you? Where are you? All of that?"

Wary, anger growing, sure he had betrayed her, she

nodded. Water gurgled against her ears.

"This building is where we do marine research. Small place and at night nobody comes here. So. Just us. Me. You. All my equipment for holding the marine life, studying it, dissecting it… knives, big hooks." He eyed her, piercingly.

She blinked. Bad, this was bad. Why was he doing this? "Why?" she whisper-gurgled.

"You killed my friend, or likely it was you? I doubt there are many mermaids in the area. My lover, my best friend, and you fuckin' killed him."

Reality dawned on her. Now she knew what that smile meant. His teeth showed. It was an evil smile. Predatory. Nasty.

"In the name of science, I'm going to study you, fillet you, dissect you, and eventually kill you. And guess what, since you are not human, nobody will give a damn."

The vehicle shifted when he vanished from view, and she heard a door open then shut, heard his footsteps.

She'd meant to die. Just not like this. Maybe… she blinked away the sudden tears, maybe this was what she deserved?

Her heart had sped up and was banging away at her chest and temples. Maybe.

The rear doors of the vehicle were flung open, one after the other, and she looked past her tail to the light, past Wolfgang to where chains hung from a high ceiling.

"Oh yes." He followed her gaze. "Those are just for hoisting specimens out of the van though. Still, it's a taste of your future. This is a Sunday, and early. About, ohhh, six AM? I have a whole day to play with you." He hauled on the end, pulled her out and let the canvas tube down onto a concrete floor. The canvas flattened, opened out.

When he kneeled beside her, she slapped her tail again, splashing him with the residual water.

Wolfgang wiped his face with one hand then grabbed her chin and dragged it around as he stared down at her. "Bitch. Was that you hating on me? I promise I do hate better than you ever could."

She tightened her jaw as he traced around her lips and made a growling sound she'd never made before.

"You're just a fucking animal. Just for you, I dug up this gag. Such sharp little teeth you have." He stroked along in front of them at the gumline. "I'm going to love your screams."

"Bashtud," she managed past the gag, and tried to fasten her teeth onto his fingers but her mouth couldn't open much more.

He pushed back on his knee and withdrew his hand, then chuckled and returned to push his fingers into her mouth and press them onto her tongue. There was a big hole in the metal rod, she realized as she choked and spluttered.

"Such a fun day ahead of us."

Then he dragged her further into the building to where there were shiny steel tables and walls lined with tanks of fish. He turned on many lights above that blinded her.

Then, while she was recovering from that, still straining to open her eyes, he hooked something into her, near where her tail muscle ended and the fin began.

Searing pain erupted.

The fire.

Rippling fire.

She gasped, held it in, tensing.

And he began to pull on a chain. It clanked as it ran through an anchor point far above, and her tail began to be hauled upward.

Her weight fell on where she was hooked.

She screamed full-throated and writhing, as he hoisted her

upward.

When he was done and she was off the floor, he left her there, swinging slightly, with her long, wet hair dragging the floor. Panting, she waited for the pain to subside a little, for the screeching feel of it running from tail to spine to her pounding head, to settle to something bearable.

Less pain, less pain…

Unscrunching her face from the grimace of agony, she heard the scrape of his boots and stared up at him. A curved knife hung point-down from one hand.

He raised it to waist-level and pursed his lips, then remained in place, stiff, uncompromising, apart from the turn of the knife as he shifted his fingers.

She couldn't help flinching. Dying by a knife, with this maniac intent on hurting her, it was going to be terrifying.

As bad as what she had inflicted on others?

Worse. At least her lovers had suffered ecstasy as well as death. Her bites had been nothing compared to steel slicing into her flesh.

She imagined the first cut of that slim weapon, her guts spilling, and pinched her teeth onto the gag. When he took a step toward her, she whimpered.

His boots crunched again, twisting in a small arc on the spot, then Wolfgang lowered himself, crouching until they were level with each other, face to face.

The knife was in his hand, glinting as he turned his wrist. The man had the eyes of the Devil, she decided. Dark, unmoving in focus, as deadly and cold as one of the great ocean predators that lurked and hunted the bigger prey. The spectacles had gone.

She whimpered again as he came even closer, until his breath met hers, then he lifted his gaze and looked up the length of her.

Blood was trickling and dripping down her, she could feel it meandering over her belly.

His mouth tightened. "Why?" The word was distorted almost beyond recognition, as if the syllables were spiked and he'd torn his throat uttering it.

Raffaela could only shake her head, minutely, not wanting to attract his attention again, fearing the knife, not sure if he wanted an answer.

"Why!" His scream was as loud as hers had been, and she shook, for it ripped into her ears. It filled the room and accused her of a multitude of things, all in that one burst of sound. Things she could never deny. The loose end of the chain above jangled at her movement.

"Why?" he said, quietly, closing his eyes, jamming them shut. The skin around his eyes furrowed. "I loved him." The sentence broke as he said it, pieces of it falling to the air as his throat again failed in its purpose.

Her shaking intensified. The chain kept rattling, signaling her fear to him. What did that matter?

This was her doing.

Even so, hate had been planted. How could it not? He hated her, and she may have detested what she had done but… the way he'd trapped her, his murderous intent, and the stench of his betrayal mingled with her fears. If she could rip out his throat, she would. Her jaw clenched, and she gnawed the rod, teeth clinging stickily to the metal.

CHAPTER FOUR

Wolfgang stood, inhaling wetly through his nose, snorting, swallowing the evidence. That was from the tears he refused to shed. His eyes would be shining with them. Roughly he dragged his arm across his face, pressing, dabbing, then he glared down at her.

Blood on her. Blood, knives, a hook through her, and that scream of hers that fair stuck a nail in his heart, ground in his worthlessness, woke him up to truth.

What was he doing?

Merrick would've laughed at Wolfgang. If he knew. If a dead man could know.

Torturing a fucking mermaid? His intent had failed at the first hurdle. This was not him.

He staggered back a small way, remembering the day Merrick was taken, and every night and day since then when he'd imagined Merrick rotting, eyeless, rolling in the waves and the currents, being picked clean by sharp-toothed fish. Fish like her. Like this hooked creature. By now, he'd be limbless and gutted.

A flesh-tattered skeleton.

All her doing. He raked her with his scrutiny again. Vengeance should have been sweet.

"What are you?"

And he wasn't sure what he was truly asking with that.

Was she human? Couldn't be.

Was she human enough to value her life as he would a human's?

He rubbed his shut eyes with splayed finger and thumb.

If she was not… what was he doing anyway? Would he torture a dolphin?

How did he prove it? Did it fucking matter? He pressed his fingers harder onto his eyeballs.

After all, when had he ever thought it moral to dissect a living animal? Never. His colleagues had laughed at him when they visited a restaurant with live lobsters in tanks. He'd walked out when they threw one, still brandishing its limbs, in a pot of boiling water.

One of his weirdnesses.

Wolfgang dropped his hands, feeling the looseness in his arms and that roiling nausea as if he might throw up. His jaw muscles knotted.

He'd stuck that gag on her to keep her from biting him with those shark teeth, maybe killing him if she reached his neck, but it also meant she couldn't talk back. What was he going to do with this lithe, beautiful, piece of death?

He kneeled again. Letting her go made him feel sick too.

Not an animal then. Too smart. A monster? So many human monsters in this world. His brain ticked over, offering up a gem of a thought for the first time in ages.

"Why do we not have fossil evidence of you, of your… *people*?" He jerked his wrist, pointing the knife at her, and his upside-down mermaid zeroed in on that with those big green eyes.

He wondered if she knew how pretty those were – how exquisite the liquid color.

Before her last visits, he'd dropped a submersible drone into the bay and had seen her coming.

She moved like a piece of wet silk through the water. Trails of the sea bubbled by in flickers that clung to her body, shreds of gemlike luminescence. Glimpses of breast and the swirling fan of dark red hair on her naked back. The undulations of her body made a liquified burlesque.

Startling. Sensual. A personification of lust.

His eyes had been open, fixed on the small cellphone screen. Absorbed, he'd almost missed looking up when she surfaced below him.

Nothing had recorded – he'd seen it, but it wasn't there. No video. No images. Nothing left on his cellphone except empty ocean. And he'd still wanted to kill her for what had been done to Merrick. Desire did not cancel hate.

He came back to the present. Grimaced at his reaction below. *Down, dick. I command you, not the other way around.*

"Why don't we see skeletons? Dead mer… folk or whatever you are? Is it magic?"

She shook her head and silver-hued tears slipped from the corners of her eyes.

Unhappy? Join the club. She probably didn't know the answer.

Wolfgang shook his head.

Did they turn into seaweed when dead? Convenient, if he were the sort who could kill her. He'd kept her asleep all day, waiting to see if that wacky folk tale were true, and had spent half those hours looking at her curled up in his sheets.

As a mermaid, underwater, she was art nouveau in motion, skin and gleaming scales and flowing hair swathed in moonlight and sea.

As a woman in his tousled sheets, she was kissable, bitable curves, her breasts tipped by soft peach-pink areolae. He'd lusted after sticking clamps on those to hear her squeals. With her legs bent high as they were, when he'd inched away the sheet, the slit of her pretty cunt showed below. Slightly swollen and with wetness glistening on the lips from their lovemaking. Tempting enough to make him stare.

Nubile, he would've thought her, as he slid his dick inside her, if she were a normal female bedmate.

And if she wasn't hundreds of years old.

Fuck this remembering her being sexy. She was here, swinging. Hooked.

Naked.

Together, he and Merrick had shared girls, upside down, tied up, doing things to them—

He squashed the painful memory, squeezed his eyes, shut, open. Not the *same* torturing a mermaid though, was it?

"Can you prove you were once a human or did you lie to me? Are you just a monster?" he rasped. *Could I prove it with tests?* "Crap," he muttered. This was his research field, and here was a perfectly fine new species. But he couldn't show her to anyone else, could he?

Not because of any moralistic fanciness. And not to spare her the scrutiny.

No. It was because he didn't want to.

Because if anyone else knew she existed it would limit what he could do to her. His cock hardened just thinking of the possibilities. He eyed the hook, the length of her and began to wonder all sorts of things…

He'd simply meant to torture her, sick man that he was. Revenge. Imagining things didn't always equal reality.

Could not. Do it. Sorry, Merrick.

Would he begrudge me thinking what I am thinking? Probably not. The man was, had been, a lecher of huge proportions. Wolfgang sighed then rested his chin on the hand bearing the knife.

This would be apt. She sang to men, then sucked them to their deaths. *Sucked them off*, to their deaths, even, maybe. He leaned in and stretched out his arm, inserted his fingers in the hole in the gag though she grimaced and tried to duck away.

Maybe he couldn't torture her to death but fucking her was not out. Studying her. While he fucked her.

"Lick. Or else this." He waved the knife. *A little terror, Merrick? Just a little* for revenge. She'd done bad things, so some repayment was in order.

When she tentatively began to lick at his fingers, he stared some more, feeling his cock grow harder, lengthen, push at his pants. He slid the knife across the floor to the side then put his unoccupied hand to her throat, grasped her there while she licked, her eyes fastened on him.

"Are you getting a stir of something? What if I give you cock instead of knife?"

Her tongue stilled, and she curved her neck. He would swear her eyes had widened.

Mermaids loved fucking men, though normally they did it for bad reasons, from what this Raffaela had said. What if… All in the name of research, he let his throat-hand run over her neck skin then up to her breasts, curved it around one and held her there, watching her as he began to play gently with her petal-soft nipple.

Her reactions, the subtle wriggles and gasps, amused him.

"Keep going," he said, guttural, thick. This was pretty depraved, but he was past wondering what he was doing. Not torturing her, that was surely a plus?

What she'd told him at the beach could be lies. Facts were

better. Human hybrid, or animal, or monster, he was still wondering which she was as he shifted and craned forward, to place his mouth over the center of her other plump breast.

His tongue followed her skin, circling, feeling the pop of her nipple erecting, and hearing a soft moan break from her mouth.

Mermaids had a thing for men, according to legend. A weakness for them.

He swirled his tongue over her now button-hard nipple then sucked, repeatedly, listening to her, feeling her body sway and arch, just a little.

The two of them were doing the most erotic of acts while she hung head-down, hooked by the tail. That had to hurt. This was damn crazy. Hand going up past her hip, he felt for her ass, only to remember she did not currently possess one. Not a human one.

Except, he felt a strangeness, a shifting, a change of whatever one might call mermaid flesh, and ass was under his hand. A fat handful of gorgeous ass on a moaning girl. He left this newly found ass, slid hand over her hip to her mound, to slide and search between her thighs, to slip along her cleft, and to stick a finger into that recently nonexistent cunt.

In… Deep…

And a miracle just when he needed one.

Sopping wet. What else on a mermaid? Her weight slewed, lopsided. She half fell, shrieking, but he caught her as he stood.

Amazed, he looked past the curve of hips and heaving taut belly, to legs. Of course there were legs. Two of, and the hook was now piercing through at her ankle.

Between the Achilles and bone, he told himself. The sight of that. He sucked on his bottom lip, wincing. *Ouch*, but she could take it.

She'd transformed, like any self-respecting mermaid would when prey was near and about to be fucked and killed by her. Wolfgang couldn't help the mild curve of his mouth. This was a bizarre, macabre event.

Man, if only he could record what he intended to do next. Still supporting her body, he unzipped and pulled out his rather magnificent erection. Much harder than the night before. That had been a chore. This was far more... fun.

Revenge fucking. If she tried to bite off his dick, she'd find it impossible.

"Keep that mouth open," he grated out. As if anything else was doable.

He could feel the rise and fall of her chest, see the puckering of her nipples, and the flush of pinkness spreading over her skin at chest and stomach – was the flush a sexual sign? He'd never seen anything that obvious on a girl. When his fingers traced up her thighs, he felt hints of where scales had been. Bluish imprints shimmered under the artificial lights.

He straightened fully, one arm around her, pulling her body up a little higher, taking the weight off the ankle hook while he grabbed his dick and searched for and found her mouth. He slid the head into the hole in the gag and found flesh, warm, yielding tongue and flesh. The saliva she'd made while sucking his finger was handy, lubricating her orifice nicely, and he wrapped his arm about her waist and hung on as he smoothly thrust in and out of her mouth.

Those teeth were locked away, though they must be human ones by now?

Nothing stopped him going deep, and he swore, grunted, and after twenty or so shoves into her, he stuck it in and remained there, fully engulfed. His eyes rolled up, as he felt her embrace the head of his dick with her pulsating throat.

That was not quite human.

God.

So immoral. So dirty. So fucking good.

Wolfgang stared down but couldn't see where he was in her, because his body was molded to hers. His mouth was close to pussy level.

Mermaids had clit, it seemed. There it was, a blatant pink-red, swollen bump where her slit began. A nodule that gleamed with wetness. He pushed his mouth over her and began to do his own sucking, a featherlight licking, nudging, pulling gently, making her stiffen and her thighs clench.

She arched into his mouth and burbled noises past his cock, bursting into a series of groans that sounded close to climax-level in joy.

He grinned, listening to her, feeling her buck at the touch of his tongue while she sucked on him. He began to do these soul-wrenching, dick-pulling small thrusts that barely left that wet hot cave of mouth. He peered up along her legs, at that hook.

A monster wasn't human.

A human didn't transform.

And was a monster a man who throat-fucked a girl with her hooked and hanging? That was a very big *yes.*

Blood trickled from her ankle wound where the hook went through.

Should he let her down? Then something odd happened below. It was as if his cock had expanded hugely, to occupy her mouth and throat in every crevice, every fold, ready to burst with come.

Enormous. The metal hole dug into him, surrounding it, squeezing him.

Throbbing, beating with his heart-blood.

He groaned terribly, unsure if it would fit out through the hole in the gag if he yanked himself from her. He might tear it off and was so fucking ready to explode in her mouth.

She sucked on him, a vacuum he had to fill, pulling him deeper, making him bigger.

She arched then shuddered, moaned onto his dick, and her throat closed in harder, tighter.

So big. So tight a space.

He shunted his cock into her and forgot where his tongue and lips were as his balls cramped and ejected his come, rocketing it into this mermaid's welcoming orifice. She was orgasming also, bucking at his mouth, pushing him back and forth then straining forward and shuddering into a rocking motion.

The chain tinkled.

He managed to extricate his cock, feeling as if he barely wrangled it out through the hole, scraping. Clenching his groin, he grunted, mind floating away. Climax totally worth it. Then he took her weight in his arms and unhooked her foot, let her down, before he staggered backward to collapse onto his butt.

Wolfgang leaned back onto his palms. The girl, the mermaid, the bleeding woman gasped at him, catching her breath, from where she lay on the floor with her arms tied at her back. Her mouth moved.

As he watched, she wriggled from her lips the crushed gag – then spat it far enough so it dangled from the leather strap, diagonally across her cheek.

The thing was mangled. His eyes surely bulged.

What. The. Fuck.

Poor quality metal.

His cock could've been in there. He glared at her.

She smiled, beatifically.

Doing anything was put on hold while he sat panting, recovering from what he had done to her and from what she had wreaked on him.

The world was no longer the same, tenets and morals were twisted, hanging off hooks about to unscrew. Sounds had ominous pretensions. The tinkles, the half-heard sighs, the repetitive taps from elsewhere might herald the arrival of a kraken, a god, a being walking in from an alternate dimension. His internal organs might have rearranged themselves for all he knew. What mysteries might he behold next?

A sonic screwdriver would be nice.

The pink flush of arousal faded from her belly.

As if an after-thought, her body shapeshifted, tail sloping, teeth popping up in a row of small knifepoints. Her tongue ran along the tops of the them, savoring the sharpness.

"Next time."

Her way of warning him? For some reason that made him chuckle.

He should have timed the change. For research more than anything.

Wiping his nose, he fumbled forward into a one-kneed position, and smiled back at her. "You'll be pleased to know, I decided not to fillet you. You're coming home with me. To live in my pool."

That shut her up.

More of a priority was deciding whether her tail needed sutures. Transformation seemed to have healed much of the hole left by the hook. The bleeding had ceased. He pushed himself off the floor and went to look more closely. Then stopped to check out her teeth, again. Her hands were still zip-tied behind her, but she might be able to arch upward.

More cautiously, he fetched his knife then circled her to

come at her tail from the back.

"Stay still."

She grumbled at him, hissed threats.

While he crouched there, pressing at the wound with his thumb, moving the now shallow laceration, deciding on the severity and what to do – antiseptic should be enough – a thought arrived.

How long? How long could he keep a mermaid? Googling that one was not going to give him an answer.

On the other hand, knowing the internet…

CHAPTER FIVE

Water spilled from the canvas as it flopped open on the flagstone edge of the pool. Carefully, Wolfgang clipped the wire at the back of her head to remove the improvised wire-and-steel gag, clipped the plastic ties on her wrists, then pushed and rolled her in. A gout of water splashed upward, and in seconds his mermaid was gliding deep then had arrived at the front wall of his pool.

Fast and efficient, swift as a shark.

He'd constructed his pool so it could be a showpiece and so he could house small sharks, if necessary.

The underwater lights decorated the aqua walls and bottom in glowing, undulating scallops of water, and she peered up at him from the bottom.

Startled by the appearance of what seemed likely a predator — and how right that assessment was — the other fish had rocketed to the wall beneath him.

He dabbled his fingertips in the pool. Did she think she could escape him down there?

Still in a squat, he reached backward and found a sun lounge, perched on it to watch her.

Beyond the edge of the pool above her, past the slope of the beach, the sun was rising out to sea, broadcasting a path of glimmers. Small breakers rolled in edged by gold. The thinner sections of wave turned to fine, dark-green glass.

The roof over the pool was fastened to the railing pillars and had been designed burglar-proof due to the isolation of his house. He'd double-checked it for strength. To reach the beach below, she'd have to bite through stainless-steel pillars and railings.

He made a mental note to cover the beach-facing glass, so that tourists and fishermen passing the bay inlet didn't see his catch swimming about.

Wolfgang scanned the water.

Still there.

Still had a mermaid in his pool.

Magic with benefits. The flick of her tail with the scales dancing in light, her areola stark as coins and reminding him of her taste and the way she bucked against his mouth when she came. Her beauty slew him, relentlessly, and he forgot to breathe.

Animal, monster, human. Her DNA would tell him?

If she were animal, he'd screwed a fish. He snorted at his thought. As if.

A pretty, pretty fish ... that made his dick so hard and big when she gave him a blowjob that he'd need new pants and a wheelbarrow for his cock and balls, if his ego had a say.

He had tidied up the room at the research facility, hosed it down, put everything away. The van could go back later, when he would swap it for his SUV, he'd left parked there. Tissue and blood samples waited downstairs, in the fridge in his kitchen. He wasn't going to leave them at work unless he was there too.

What would those show? What she had told him said she

was human, once, but he was no lie detector. She might tell him anything. The honesty of mermaids was not proclaimed in tales, only their shipwrecking and seduction skills.

His house, he remembered, was a mess. Except for where he'd walked her, yesterday. The reason for that smacked home how crazy he was being. To dismiss his vengeance and end up with her in his tank was a rebound of enormous proportions.

When Merrick died, grief had buried him.

Once upon a time, they'd sat here together, drinking wine, laughing, eating pâte, cheese, and antipasto. But Merrick was gone, dead, killed by her or her ilk. And yet that bludgeoning ache of grief had dulled from an obliteration of his very self to *this*, to acceptance, in one night?

His eyeballs felt raked, desiccated, and very tired. He'd not slept in how long? No idea. Perhaps he'd blown some sort of mental fuse. Denial, anger, grief, acceptance. Were those the stages? Vengeance didn't get a mention.

Between his legs, he drummed the rim of the sun lounge.

Okay, so maybe he wasn't going to kill her. Wolfgang scrubbed at his chin with his fingers, staring down at her, but this?

"What did you do to me?"

Mermaids and sirens seduced men with song, but he had to admit the rest of her seduced him purely by being in front of him. If she had somehow done that, then she'd encouraged her own violation. Ironic, since he thought he was in command. Unless seduction was automatic and a mechanism she didn't control?

An interesting way to look at it. Generally speaking, he could resist a woman in a short skirt in a dark alley at night. How a woman dressed would turn him on but not compel him.

But a mermaid had a supernatural essence.

Had she made him do it despite her protestations?

Or was that irrelevant due to his plans to dissect her? His head hurt.

"Your honor, I fucked her because her siren beauty made me do it." He tsked. Not sure that would work in court. A pity. Fatigue crept in and thumped him again, weighing down his body and making scratchy eyeballs even scratchier.

"Ohhh god." Groaning at the headache prying him apart, he rose to his feet. He would clean up his house and think on this. Crash into bed. Pray she didn't get out and come and drown him, somehow, in his bed. Maybe by sitting on his face.

Chuckling at his vile humor, he staggered toward the stairs that led down to the door, which then led past his main lounge room.

Wait. What was he going to feed her?

She must eat something more than people? A splash made him halt, and he turned. Raffaela had surfaced.

"What do you eat?" Then he saw the wriggling fish in her hands, the chunk missing from its middle, and the blood staining the water. "Okay. Right. Now I know. Hungry, were you?"

Narrow-eyed, she nodded then bit off more fish, chewed.

His pool filters could handle the blood and debris.

Blood smeared her lips.

Something induced him to return to the pool. Easier to talk with less distance. If she lunged from the other side he had, *ohhh*, about three seconds to get away? Wolfgang took one step back. Make that four.

"Was it you? Did you drown my lover, my Merrick?" Had to know. *Had to.* "He was—"

"Yes, it was me," she snapped. "I remember his name. I

heard it when you called to him, as he slipped under the sea with me. I remember the feel of him inside me. His kisses." Then she halted, expression faltering.

She'd been taunting him. It had been working. He inhaled, stifled his need to hurt her. "Go on."

Her mouth twisted, and she lowered the dead fish beneath the water. She spoke again, her voice softened, "I did try to save him. He was haunting, he was *different* from the others. Something about him made me try to make him come alive, again, even after. You know? I'm sorry."

Water dripped.

"So very sorry."

Not just because he'd aimed to knife her?

He grunted, off balance, anger simmering but not quite erupting. *Sorry.* What did you do when your lover's murderer said sorry?

Spit on them? Scream? Knife them anyway? He was staring at her bobbing tits where they showed above the pool surface, with the stirred water sloshing over them. *Fuck them hard, without remorse?*

Get vengeance on them some other way?

His face would shatter if he stayed a second more, and so he turned away and jogged down the stairs. He spent the next hours cleaning the house, sorting things. He filled the trash can to overflowing, then put away the broom and vacuum, and went to Merrick's room, which had become more of a storage and playroom when he moved into the main bedroom.

He hadn't been in here since the day the man had gone missing.

The death certificate was still coming. They didn't like issuing those without proof of death. Without a body.

Wolfgang lay down on the bed and stayed there, still,

hollow, staring at the walls, at the ceiling.

The neat display of kink gear on the walls taunted him. The floggers and leather harnesses. The chains, clamps, dildos, arm restraints, shackles, and masks. An entire kink shop's worth of BDSM accessories was going to waste.

"I need you man. I so fucking need you. What would you do with her?"

He'd probably say do anything you want to. Merrick had a wildness to him. That last night, the night before the day he vanish—

Stop thinking about him. Stop. Thinking.

No more memories. None.

He made himself do math in his head, wonder what the weather was like, and decide who would win the next election. Also why people counted sheep.

He fell into sleep at some point, a nightmarish running-away-from-everything, falling-off-a-cliff-into-a bottomless-sea sort of sleep.

When he woke, he hadn't moved on the bed, and every part of his body felt as stiff as if he'd been working in a labor camp building the pyramids, or something even bigger.

Cursing, he dragged himself upright. At least he hadn't been drowned by mermaid pussy.

His cellphone had messages, and the time, date. Strangely it was still Sunday.

Two in the afternoon? He could get into the lab and check her blood, package up the tissue to send it away for testing. They couldn't do DNA properly at the Trantor Marine Institute.

Except that when he opened the fridge and checked, the specimens had turned to water and some sort of black sludge. Extract of seaweed was actually a distinct possibility.

Minuses – no DNA test could be performed. Pluses? He

could kill her, dump her body in front of the cops, and nobody would ever find him guilty.

Wolfgang hesitated at the thought of going to see her. He'd leave her be, for a while.

Three days passed. Sitting on the sofa in the darkened living room, he drank beer, ate snacks, and watched her swim in his pool and consume all of his fish. The pool was brightly lit by sun in the daytime and the pool lights at night. She could not see him watching her.

He considered jerking off but didn't. Thoughts revolved and evolved. No images would stay of her on any devices, but he could make notes of any discoveries.

Getting more living fish wasn't easy. Or not *that* easy. As from tomorrow, he was on official leave for a month because of Merrick. Taking specimens from the facility would get him reprimanded, and he meant to return to work once he was done with mindfucking this mermaid. Something from the fishmonger would do.

He thought about that, about her food, for two days before he did something.

Found some ancient scotch whisky in his cellar, sat on the sofa, and then he eyed her through the glass of his tumbler, swirling it, kissing the cold side.

Now she looked hungry.

Raffaela wasn't dumb. She had somehow figured out where he was located, and she swam up to the glass. She plastered her hands to it to either side, shadowing her eyes, and peered through.

Their eyes seemed to connect. She showed her teeth, and he raised the scotch in the tumbler to her.

A hungry mermaid might be more dangerous or more malleable.

Malleable was his aim.

Vengeance, another way. Yes. Wolfgang smiled. He was going to enjoy this.

With that decision made, tamped down, cemented in, he felt as if he were finally honoring Merrick's memory.

He left her another two days to be sure she would be extra hungry then went to see her. In one hand, he carried a duffel bag containing a pistol, a new steel gag, rope, and handcuffs. In his other was a plastic bag with two fresh but dead fish. He opened the frosted-glass door and jogged up the stairs that led to the pool.

CHAPTER SIX

Since he'd lowered a cover over the outside of the pool glass, Raffaela could no longer see the beach, the sand, or the waves, though she could hear the muted roar, smell the salt, hear the calls of the sea birds. Reflections of sunlight rippled through the white canvas cover and onto the sand beneath her. Plants familiar to her swayed below, green and healthy, a replica of life in the shallower parts of the sea. Rocks, sand, plants, and the hum of some machine that pushed clean water from holes in the walls.

It was not enough. A longing to return to the ocean had become constant and had strengthened over the last few days. She did not wish to die. Not anymore. The ire of this vile man had enervated her. He'd tricked her, trapped her.

At first, she had been sorry.

Now she was angry at him for wanting to cut her up. He thought she was the monster?

It was he.

The ocean was her home. Her human past was centuries ago. She would have climbed out and torn her way to the sea if it were possible. Reach the beach, then she would roll and squirm back into the water.

But she'd tried to get out and could not.

Her teeth had made only the mildest of scratches on the bars surrounding the pool.

Instead of escaping, she was resigned to swimming back and forth in the water allowed her. Nothing kept her company – not since she'd eaten the last of the fish. Nothing except for a few seagulls and sparrows that ventured inside to perch on the railings or furniture and look down at her.

And him. And Wolfgang.

She could tell when he watched. He stopped the lights working inside the house when he did so. It made the glass darken and reflect the light from out here… unless she swam up to it.

And yet he did not feed her, even though he'd asked what she ate and must see there was nothing left. It made her wonder if he'd decided to let her starve to death.

She was floating on her back, watching the latest sparrow do circuits above her, catching bugs perhaps, when…

The door he'd last left through made a *click*. The mechanism sighed then it sounded as if the door had closed again. She'd wriggled over the tiles to look at that door a few times. She sat up, listened. Then she heard his feet coming up the steps. Bare feet, sticking to the floor.

She slipped across to the front wall of the pool to be as far from him as possible.

"Hello there! I've brought you food." He raised what seemed a large bubble of water with fish stuck to the insides.

A plastic bag they called those. She'd swum through enough in the sea, along with all the other garbage that came from humans.

Dark gray pants on him today, and a form-fitting white shirt clung to the broad muscles of his chest. As he looked down at her the black curls of his hair hung before his dark eyes and darker eyebrows, and he'd walked up those stairs with the swagger of a confident man. She imagined sliding her arms down those big masculine thighs.

The man was pretty, and she would lay a wager he knew it.

Food. He'd said food.

Her stomach protested, rumbling.

While she stared, he deposited a large, long brown bag on a seat. It clinked and he unfastened an opening, then removed several objects. Shiny handcuffs emerged then rope, and she recognized another gag. Her mouth twinged as she remembered how the last one had felt. Her mouth had bled afterward. She clung to the pool wall, sinking, molding her back to it, revealing only her eyes above the water.

And there was a gun. The form of it was as far removed from the look of the guns of her time as was a sailing ship from the vessels that plied the present oceans, but she knew it. A pistol.

She feared his intent but summoned courage, surfaced higher so her mouth was above the surface.

"Will you feed me or starve me? I will not submit to that again." She nodded at the devices.

Gun in hand, he sat in one of the long, white seats then casually rested the weapon on his knee.

"I am taking precautions."

She angled an eyebrow.

"You are more a danger to me, currently, than I am to you. Raffaela."

He recalled her name.

"You said you would cut me up. I doubt your words."

"True. I did. And you know my reasons. I didn't cut you. I have backtracked. I want to keep you. I said that too."

He had.

"I cannot live forever in a small pool of water." Or without enough food. She smelled the fish, and again her stomach cramped.

"Perhaps. It would be boring, but one cannot die from boredom. Besides, I have ideas, surprises. Notions about you. What if you could walk about my house?"

Startled, she blinked at him and sank to the bottom to think before she returned. "How?"

"I would have to demonstrate and try things. As long as you admit it is sensible for me to restrain you to begin with? You have such sharp…" He indicated her. "Teeth. You could rip my head from my neck, and maybe my beating heart from my chest with those."

She favored him with a glimpse of her teeth.

These ideas made her nervous. But if she did not agree, what would he do? Fillet her after all? She needed time, and if she could get into the house below, she might escape through another door.

Houses had many doors, from memory. She hadn't been inside a building for more than a century. The noises coming from pubs and cafés and whatever else she had walked by on her day on land, those frightened her. The yelling, the singing, and the banging, even the loud talking, it hurt her ears, made her heartbeat pound.

Which made her wonder why she wanted to become human again. It would be nice, in small bits. Maybe? If it were her choice as to when and where.

"And so. This." He raised the gun. "And these. Submit to the restraints and we will talk, and experiments can be done on you to see about the walking." He eyed her intently, smiling as if he knew a secret. "Then, if I think you're safe, I will let you loose, more and more."

That sounded fair, if dangerous. Was he lying again? She remembered lies too. People loved those. He could easily kill her.

He could do that here, in the pool. Not feed her. Poison her. Harpoon her. Those she'd seen used far too often. Her people, her ex-people, were good at making war and weapons.

Which way to go? Staying in the pool would get her nowhere.

"You can help me walk?"

He shrugged. "Maybe. How many mermaids do you think I've had in my hands?"

The pump that fed water to the pool hummed in the background.

"Perhaps this could be satisfactory." Frowning, she thought some more. Experiments? She had heard of the Frankenstein experiment, and there had been stories of other things. Long ago, those tales were told, but were they true or fairy tales?

"There will be a price to pay."

"What price?" Dread tingled through her. He didn't mean to cut her up?

"Pleasure in exchange for freedom." He leaned forward. "You want to walk again?"

Oh. She understood. *What pleasures,* might be a question an innocent would ask, but she knew the answer. The man had sexual inclinations.

Was that so awful? Only if he planned to hook her through the tail to do it.

The alternatives were starvation, boredom, and eventual death. Choice was lacking. The open ocean and the cycle of the Ravening now seemed a dream to her, not a nightmare.

To make her walk, he would need to conjure up legs. To

have legs, she had to be human.

If she were human, she could have a life on land.

Could she yearn for both sea and land, at once? To choose between them on a whimsy? *Yes, yes.* One was an achievable goal, the other a fantasy she would love to make come true.

"If you are lying—"

"I am not. It's just that this will be a new, exciting, and unpredictable science. If it is science? If magic, I'm no expert on that."

Hmph.

She nodded. "I will agree then. Yes." A thought arrived. "No hooks?"

No knives, her mind pushed at her, but she decided not to say it.

"No. No hooks." He smiled at her with that familiar flat-eyed smile.

That had not changed. Somehow, she thought he was deceiving her, but how? Why even?

"So, I have a yes. Good."

He threw a fish to her and she consumed it in seconds, gulping it down, ripping it apart, the blood cloud spreading. Then he tossed the gag at her. It hit the water a few feet away and sank.

"Fasten that in your mouth, firmly, do not pretend and make it loose or I will be angry." He flourished the gun, aiming it at her. "It will click shut at the back. After it's on, swim to me."

What else could she do but dive and pick it up, fit it to herself, then swim to him?

Wrong, so very wrong to trust him.

But she had decided. This was a more open choice than swimming back and forth in the pool.

He kept the gun aimed at her forehead as she swam closer.

"Good little mermaid. Get up here."

That seemed to amuse him, and she glowered.

He patted the tiles beside him and backed away. "Sit on the edge of the pool, facing the sea and put your hands at your back."

What? She hesitated.

"You are, to put it lightly, a killing machine. Win my trust and we can do away with the handcuffs."

"I am not a kill—" She tried to say indignantly, through the gag. It came out garbled. He got the message. It would be obvious.

"I saw what you did to Merrick. How am I supposed to know when this Ravening hits?"

She would tell him… but he would not believe that. And truthfully, maybe she would not.

And so, reluctantly, while glowering, she raised herself and sat on the edge of the pool and let him handcuff her.

His large hand arrived on her shoulder and stayed there while she listened to his breathing, to the shuffling as he kneeled behind her, and she wondered why she was trusting him.

Because, what else? A killing machine was not her norm, not until the Ravening came, and surely that was not due for some time? It was not predictable, but far more than a month separated her episodes of luring and drowning men. She shivered as his hand moved, and he murmured.

"You are behaving for me, so well. I am impressed."

That seemed almost an insult.

Then he leaned over and kissed her, even though the gag was partly in the way. The touch of a man was a rare thing in her life. Sometimes she forgot how nice it felt to have a mouth on hers. Pushing her around, moving her with the weight of him behind that mouth. She had shut her eyes at the first press and was simply enjoying the spread of heat.

When he smoothed his hand all over her skin as he kissed, she felt herself softening, melting.

Kissing was a form of love.

She craved this and whimpered as he kept up the massage, summoning the restoration of lust, thrumming its way…

Down her body…

Then she knew.

What he intended.

The reasons for arousing her.

The shift happened in a mindless chasm. In a blink. A tumult.

One minute, mermaid…

The next, she was sprawled on her back, legs still in the pool, with him over her, body up the other way so he seemed upside down for a second until she had herself oriented properly. He breathed as heavily as she did.

"Well, now." He wiped his mouth with the back of his hand. "That was easy, my little…" He inhaled again. "Fuck, you are something, even before you change. I swear my balls and dick do weird things."

Wide of eye, unblinking, she watched as he lowered himself to his elbows to kiss her again, upside-down kisses.

Oh," she whispered, into his mouth, as both his hands covered her breasts and played with her there. She tried to arch into his hold, even when he increased the pressure of his fingers and pushed her flat.

How did this man send such a thrill through her when she was trapped and worried, and… *whatever.* She gave up on thinking.

He shifted, pressing his kisses lower, lower, down and over the length of her, until he reached her pussy. Raffaela was much of the way to nirvana, fingers clasped at her back, writing a little and wishing he would put himself into her mouth, because she wouldn't bite his dick, would she?

And then he took his weight from her, rolled away.

He pulled her completely from the pool, flipped her onto her belly, and tied her legs together with the skinny bits of black plastic he'd once had on her wrists. Those cut. They hurt if she yanked at them.

If she could have spoken properly, she'd have said something startled, a curse. Instead she only squealed when he bit her ass.

Then… *then*, he pried apart her butt cheeks and probed her.

Instinctively she tried to thrash her tail, and only knocked his foot. He pinned her down with a knee to her ass.

No tail was there. Her jaws were strong, she was stronger than any mere human girl, but she had no tail, no sharp teeth, and he was doing things she did *not* approve of. His finger circled her bottom hole as if it fascinated him. No man had ever done this.

Nor should he. She growled past the gag, disappointed that this new metal was far too tough for her to mash.

CHAPTER SEVEN

Wolfgang laughed quietly. Those little growling noises she was making as he fingered her asshole were cute and only made his dick harder. Not surprising.

He'd always had a thing for girls who struggled.

He worked his fingertip into her. There was lube on his finger, so she really had no reason for complaint, considering.

"You agreed. To exchanging my pleasure for a chance to see if I can give you legs, make you human. You know?"

As he switched out his finger for the smallest of the butt plugs he'd fetched from the bag, revolving it as he slipped it inside her, he eyed the length of her newly formed legs. The pearlescent outlines where scales had been. The black ties around her ankles, doubled up because she could probably kick like a mu… like a girl who had recently possessed a tail that let her zip fifty yards in seconds.

Already, his leg had a bruise.

This was not normal.

He widened his eyes, looked to where he had his hand

over her butt, squeezed her there to get another squeak from her. The scale impressions or illusionary markings faded out just about where his hand was resting. The head of the butt plug showed.

Hieronymus Bosch would go *pffft* and had likely painted madder than this while picking his teeth.

But surreal was a completely inadequate description.

She blew away his dreams, surpassed every other female who had ever occupied his bed, or his and Merrick's, or his wall.

And the way she took that plug said fucking her there would happen soon. Not a work-his-way-up-the-size-scale for days thing. He kissed the underside of one cheek, then bit, squeezing his hand under her to find her clit. Though he'd been fixed on her as if she were under his microscope, the shift had blurred his vision. One second, she was a mermaid with a tail, and then she was this.

He bit her plump ass again, moved up her length kissing and biting. The smaller yelps, her sighs, the faint redness on her back, it told him she was at least enjoying what he was doing.

Taking off that gag pulled at him. He could. Just, he had an aversion to having his life blood draining away onto the floor from a gap in his neck.

When he reached her neck, he gave her nape a good firm bite, hung onto the muscle at the side, felt the shudder of her body.

She likes.

Too easy. He wanted more protesting. More fury. Getting the balance correct between turned on and seriously annoyed was going to be curious.

"How are we doing?" He sprawled himself beside her on the pool tiles, on a level with her one eye that showed as she peeked sideways. She worked her lips on the gag. Wolfgang ran his knuckles along her chin, leaning in and turning her head then kissing the corner of her mouth.

"Sorry. I am not going to take that off." Not enough courage.

But also, he kind of liked girls gagged, until he wanted to force a BJ from them. Or something else. Oh the habits Merrick had reinforced in him. Switching on each other, training girls. Together they'd made good use of all that kink gear.

Shut up, he told his memory, feeling the happy drain away. *Shut. Up.*

He ducked his head into her shoulder, smelling her, calming himself.

No remembering, especially not now, when he had her all tied up.

His vengeance seemed pettier than ever. His years of education, the hours he had spent learning the intricacies of evolution, cellular biology, reproduction, all blown away by her going from what she had been to this. This was a revolutionary discovery, and he…

He wanted. To fuck around with her. Because she'd killed his lover.

Torturing a mermaid? Petty as fuck.

Accept it. Life had devolved to this. He was petty. He was too fascinated and pissed off to write this up to get accolades, or to display her as he lectured on the physiology of mermaids.

He nudged her neck with his nose, bit her again, let go, nibbled up her jawline while he watched and listened. Her eyelids fluttered. Drool shone on the gag.

"Our experiment is going well. You have legs."

Raffaela grunted at him, nose wrinkling.

"Even better, I have a pussy I can fuck. A mermaid shifted so I can toy with her how I like." He grinned. Messing with her, causing unease, all par for the course.

Why would he want her entirely happy?

A thought occurred. Arousal made her shift. If she lost that and shifted back when her legs were tied apart, it could be mayhem.

Note to self. Keep that in mind.

He flipped her over again, applied himself to eating out her pussy for a few minutes until she was looking close to coming. Cuteness personified, all that straining and squirming. Then he rose, wiped his mouth, and picked her up in his arms.

Cuddling her to his chest, he adjusted his hold and headed for the door.

What a nice bundle. His cock was throbbing at the thought of what he could do next.

"Time to fuck a girl. Where will I start? In the ass? Hmmm?"

She glared up at him.

He tsked. "You killed someone I love. What did you expect? I get to mess with you, as well as give you legs. How long do you think we can keep this up for?"

The flush on her chest was probably a giveaway.

He maneuvered down the steps, turned and used his butt to push down the door handle, shoved the door fully open, and went through sideways.

How in hell was he to take notes on her reactions while he edged her?

He looked down at his mildly annoyed mermaid, and along her body, to her legs, her mons, her thighs, and the curves went everywhere they should, and more. He felt a surge of awe and his anticipation rise to mammoth heights, along with his cock pretending it could burst his zipper.

"Christ!" He tried to wriggle as he walked toward the sofa, so as to rearrange things.

Barely touched her and this? He wanted her badly. Could feel the slide of dick going in. Those big eyes watching him.

Anything, he could do anything, and she was not an ordinary female. Not known to anyone else. She was his for as long as he could keep her a secret and alive.

His. To do what he wanted with.

Excruciating.

He took the last few steps fast, laid her on the floor, unzipped, turned her to remove that ass plug, then managed to stick himself into her asshole for an inch. The shove to penetrate her was not fast but not super-slow either.

He was going to explode already. What was it with mermaids?

Siren. Remember? They have special… fucking goddam properties. Especially the fucking.

Wolfgang grunted as he thrust into her in small increments, sweat on his brow, trickling. Squeezed in, forced in a smidgen further, held it, and…

Jaw clamping, he came in a gush, in a rhythmic pump of cum that flooded mostly outside of her. His hands grasped either side of her hips, and he held on, feeling the downslide of ecstasy.

Damn. He needed to train himself more than her.

Though training her too would be awesome. All the chains and collars could get used again.

His cock began to swell, and despite the brief mini-agony of gaining an erection so soon after a climax, it was hardening.

Her? He looked down at his messy cum-splattered mermaid. She seemed very still, tongue licking out through the gag. If anything, the flush of red on her back had increased. Were the two of them in some sort of echoing empathic situation here?

"Was that a turn-on?"

He put two fingers together and slowly wormed them into her barely used hole, and saw her eyes slam shut, and a sigh come from those pretty lips.

Well. Noteworthy. Very much so.

CHAPTER EIGHT

Raffaela gave an embarrassed whimper as he withdrew his fingers. Men had disgusting habits when it came to sex, but this was one she'd never had to cater for when human. That it felt… interesting only mildly improved this situation.

The ass was surely a taboo place on anyone, yet the feel of his fingers inside her lingered.

"I see you liked that."

Smug man. She glared, hating on him some more. Letting herself die had slipped to last on her list of things to do. Mutilating him should be first.

When he walked away, she decided to stay where she lay. Rolling over would accomplish nothing.

Somewhere in the house, water was running. Water, the subtle, forever caress and tickle of it as she swam, surrounding her, holding her. The sound had taken her back to her world.

She was pining for the sea.

When he returned, he turned her over, placed his mouth on her at the join of her legs and his palm on her just above, holding her in place. Arousal thrummed, a hard torrent of pleasure she could not resist – not while his tongue moved on her.

When he raised his head, her moisture wet his face.

How wet she'd become. Panting, she stared down at him, and tried to speak. The gag stopped her.

Frustrating. She flopped back her head to the floor. Her breath rasped loudly through her open mouth.

"Stay still and remember I have a gun." He waved it.

He was so afraid of her. Or did he merely love to make threats?

Turned over and face-down, she closed her eyes, wondering what he was up to next. He untied her ankles and she tensed. Wolfgang stuck the muzzle of the gun into her butt, slowly letting it slide down until the gun was…

Until he…

Where was he going?

He inserted it between her cheeks then found her entrance, worked the weapon up and down as he held her open with his fingers.

"Fuck. That's hot."

Raffaela twisted, gaped at him. The thought of him pulling the trigger was scary, daunting, but gods, yes, the danger also stirred her.

Ridiculous that she reacted so.

Death was not what it once had been. It was a known thing. A daily presence. Whereas this, being slowly fucked by a pistol, was new.

He slid it deeper, and she hid her face, hid the sounds she made.

"That, halfway in you… Damn. I'll have to clean it now." More blushing occurred, and she wriggled, bleated – which only made the gun move inside her. "Stay still."

The gun was removed, though, and she relaxed.

Her wrists were unlocked and he began to do something with rope — tying first one wrist to its nearest ankle and making her rise on her knees.

She could have objected. Could have tried to jump him. He'd made her curious with his devotion to violating her. This wasn't vengeance anymore.

Both of them were changing, delving into something profoundly sexual — a depravity she'd never thought existed.

The way he pleasured her, feeling her, holding her hair in his lock-fingered grip, gathering it with delicious pain while he kissed her, everywhere. She pretended it was not her doing the moaning.

An ex-whore knew of things. There were men who liked taboo ass play. Men who liked spanking. But tying girls up in intricate knots? After so long being lonely and only taking prey when it was demanded of her by the Ravening, this was interesting.

More than interesting. It was spellbinding.

It distracted her, to be so expertly *handled*. He knew how to tie a woman, and that was not something one learned on the spot. Aware that his threats might hold some truth, she allowed everything to happen.

He had a gun, but her female parts were fairly singing at her in chorus.

She searched her mind, backtracking through the swirl of her responses, and came to a revelation. She could sense his ardency like a shark tasting blood on the water, miles from the violence.

Siren. We are siren, her mind whispered. *Yes. That's it.* He was right to fear her. Her true strength was not her teeth.

She ended up with each wrist tied to its equivalent ankle but separated from the other wrist and ankle. He stood and patted her head, fisted her hair, and craned back her neck so they must meet, eye to eye.

"There. Now my pretty girl…" he murmured to her ear, with brushes of soft lips – a beguiling contrast to the pains in her scalp from his twining fingers.

She wanted to squeeze her thighs together but couldn't.

Girl though? Oh, she liked that. A lot. It said she was more than monster

"We'll watch some TV and see how long I can keep you turned on, while you sit on my lap on the sofa."

He swiveled her, rearranging her as if she were a doll kneeling on a mantlepiece, and pointed at two padded seats. They were long and formed into a deep U-shape due to being pushed close to each other. Both were rich brown in color.

He left her alone for a moment, padding away.

This room, one entire wall of this room, was the glass of her tank. Sun streamed through the water.

Green, the sun turned it into a perfect clarified green, with the sand lined up and snuggled against the glass.

Water was her element. Her rightful place. Then what was she doing here?

Being his little doll toy. *Mmm.*

His idea for making her human was to make her shift due to pleasure. If he'd asked, she could have told him it would wear off.

However, what was a TV? Left on her knees on the floor rug, she followed him, brow wrinkling, as he picked up a small black rectangle and pressed on it. The gun lay discarded on a low, shiny metal table beside the sofas.

Everything was shiny.

On the wall adjacent to the pool wall, a rectangle of black became a talking, moving picture.

TV.

She chewed on the gag.

Oh. Oh yes. She'd seen these through the huge windows of establishments that were thronging with rowdy people. Or in the windows of shops. The years had flicked by, one after another, and she would walk in the towns. Each year the TVs grew bigger, brighter, until they seemed a cut-out part of life, made loud and flat.

Television they had called them, once. TV now.

Wolfgang tossed the rectangle aside, strode to her then kissed her. He surely loved kissing. Her mouth hurt after all this time wrenched apart, and she winced.

"Huh." He examined her, his fingers exploring along her gumline. "Human teeth. Good. But I bet you can still crush my dick with these." His mouth twisted at the corner. "I bet."

Somehow that sounded… Wistful.

"You are so… You make me want to touch you."

His hands ran over her, traveling skin on skin, murmuring thrills, summoning passion.

These fleeting touches conjured frissons, a trail of his fingers that made her shiver and gasp, tantalizing her at neck, ears, and breasts, tickling over her stomach. He seemed to marvel at what he found at times, and he bent and kissed her lightly like a supplicant priest.

Slowly he straightened. Wolfgang stepped away, breathing as hard as she.

He hesitated before he spoke, his hands curling up, closing.

"I'm going to take off the gag. You're not to bite me." That was said as if he wasn't sure it would happen like he wanted but was past caring. "I want to hear you speak, the sounds you make—"

He glowered at her with his head tilted low.

Eyebrows raised, she found herself trembling. Stuck on her knees, tied up, and he was acting as if she had made him do this. She was something no one had catalogued or studied or, thankfully, dissected. *Siren. Maybe, this was my doing?* The thought sang to her and she smiled to herself. And what siren would refuse such mad devotion?

None.

She wasn't sure if she would bite him under any circumstances. Not now.

Her need to mutilate him horrendously had been obliterated.

She needed him to touch her again. *Needed*, not wanted. Compulsion.

Even so. People bit too. Raffaela traced her tongue around the inside of the gag metal. She could've done it as a human girl. Dicks were not made of rock, no matter that men boasted of such. Some of her patrons in the streets of London had liked her biting them as they fucked her mouth.

"So. No biting. Okay?"

She nodded. Anything to get this thing off.

The gag was removed and placed beside the gun, then he stepped away and undressed. His hands were trembling, but his cock was fully erect.

So soon. That was not normal for a man.

She'd never tested her siren powers on land or when the Ravening was not on her.

"What are you doing to me?"

He leaned in and thumbed her neck on her beating pulse.

"You will see. Be good." Desperation in that tone, passion in his hold. He pushed up her head, angled his own, and kissed her, this one hard and somehow grim. Determined kissing. Lips roved on lips, tugging, nipping, breathing each other's air and delicate moans, and his tongue ventured into her mouth.

It was a torrid possession, a physical love with a care to arouse her that she'd not had before. Not ever. Her human life had been short, horrible, and minus love, once her mother died, unless you counted whoring.

No longer in charge of anyone's death, unfettered from her cyclical compulsions, she let herself unravel and simply…

Be.

The kiss evolved, roamed, his mouth tasting at her lower, lower, at breast and underside, turning her nipples into small jutting rocks. His hands were on her, in her, delving into mouth and sliding over her, finding her cunt. She felt *used* and he'd barely done more than…

Well.

Well, he had come inside her asshole.

Not the same. Not enough. She shuddered as he bit the inside of her thigh and licked her there.

"Your clit is up and ready, like my cock.

"Clit?" She was confused. The words he used—

"This." Lightly he bit her beside the button where her arousal centered. It brought a yelp from her, a flinch, and he laughed against her skin.

"More," she croaked, groaning at the wet, soft heat of tongue and lips.

On her private parts. Raffaela arched. *Oh. My. God.*

His tongue wormed along the forepart of her slit.

Arching made her hands hurt at the wrists. Rope had her. *He* had her, and she moaned again, compelled by this attention.

Men did not do this, did not lick at her until she shook with desire.

"Want me?" he asked, teasing her again. "Inside you. Fucking you."

Her pussy spasmed in at the thought of him fucking her.

She peered at him and made a strangled sound that said *yes*, or she thought it should.

"Come." He stood then picked her up, carefully balancing her body in his arms, and he kissed her as he walked.

They ended up before the sofa, the TV on but ignored. Wolfgang lowered himself to the sofa and seated her over him. She had no choice in how he positioned her, her arms were at her sides and bound to ankles, her legs resting on the sofa and parted over him.

Over his cock. She looked down, fascinated, her pussy throbbing, pulsing it seemed to her heartbeat.

"See." He wrapped his fist around it and eyed her. "You're fucking turned on and still shifted to human. I might point out that shifting back right now would give your tail schizophrenia, but to hell with that. I want to spear you on my cock. *Down*."

His fist tightened on his erection, and he shuffled her forward on his lap, her lower legs sliding on the leather. Shiny leather that gave under their weight. She sucked at her lip as she felt his cock probing her entrance, pushing upward.

And she threw back her head, feeling him enter her, his hands on her hips forcing her lower.

"Fuck," he blurted as she felt his fingers explore below, where his cock tunneled, and her aroused wetness made them slide. Laughing, he added, "Are all mermaids this fucking wet?" He shoved higher. The push and tightness made her shriek and grab her ankles with rigid fingers.

"Fuck!" Said more softly, and Wolfgang jerked his hips and stuck himself inches deeper.

Every fraction of him was tangible, every throb, every

stretch of her walls. The tight fit of cock to cunt squeezed out liquids, dripping, from inside her onto her thighs.

Up and down that slippery, violating cock. Grunting, Wolfgang showed his teeth when she dared to look at him, or at lower where they were joined. She was rocked, slammed at, made to gasp and squirm.

Then, on a down thrust, half-out, he stopped, groaned, held her in place.

"What?" she spluttered, catching up to breathing, striving to make him enter her fully. "Keep going." At the twitch and swell of him, her eyelids shut.

"Enough." With a hip movement and a grasp to either side of her butt, he lifted her off him.

Dismayed, she pouted as his cock sprang free between them.

"Not yet. You are not allowed." He sucked in a breath, eyed her. "Experiment, remember? Though—"

With some difficulty he deposited her on her knees on the floor then edged forward on the sofa until his cock head nudged her shut mouth.

Glowering she pouted again.

"Oh, you will. Or else. I have so many things I can use on you. Open and suck on me."

Raffaela shook her head.

"You'll shift if I stop playing with you or let you come too soon. You will wait." Hands either side of her face, he touched forehead to forehead and said quietly, "Experiment. What if you could walk about all day?"

"But only if I'm horny as a goat?"

He slipped a hand between her legs, swiped along her slit and his hand came up shiny. He showed her then went back to toying with her. "You're dripping. I'm going to fuck you hard on every surface in this house. Is that such a chore?"

The room swayed, and she inhaled sharply, picturing herself being fucked, bent over, on the rug, against a wall. She clutched at air, tensing her hands, closing them. "No?"

"See."

He pushed her down again and swore when his cock unexpectedly touched her protruding tongue. Staring he watched as she licked partway around the edge of the cap then up to the very tip.

"Holy…" Wolfgang shoved himself forward.

He almost came in her mouth again but stopped and brought her up to sit over his lap again, only this time she faced the TV. With no warning, he penetrated her, pushing her body down. He seemed balls deep in an instant.

Her head dropped forward. So good.

With him rocking in and out of her, bouncing her up and down, she missed seeing whatever was on the TV, only to deliriously beg him to keep going when he inevitably stopped.

"Oh. Oh no. Please?"

Face red, sweat dribbling, Wolfgang twisted her to look at him and stared. His gaze was stern, ungiving. Which reminded her on the iron-hard cock shoved inside her. Her pussy lips seemed welded around his shaft.

She moved infinitesimally and made a pitiful noise.

"Hey. No. What if you come and then shift after?"

"I don't care. Please?" She was begging. Worth it, so worth it.

He pulled out but hoisted her face down onto the sofa, then speared into her, fully, nailing her down over and over, bumping her face into a cushion, making her turn her head to breathe.

Deafened by her own moans and mewling sounds, she gave a strangled gasp and felt him come, again, jerking into her, jammed up, molded to her, his last spurts a reminder he was done.

She muttered threats as he withdrew.

More, she needed, more. Whatever abilities she had to compel him were affecting her also. It was painful to need so direly. With the Ravening, she would climax in unison with the man, revel in his death, bask in the glow of life.

This was different.

He buried his face in her neck then collapsed to the sofa beside her. "I've never come so fast so many times… You're making me want to screw you to infinity, and that movie reference should get me committed."

With his eyes shut, he didn't see her wriggle closer and move in to lick at his ear, to whisper sweet encouragement. In her words and the rise and fall of her voice, she recognized a quiet rhythm. It was not song, or music. Too subtle for that.

The needs of a siren were not to be denied. Even tied up, she had her ways.

Wolfgang moaned. He edged forward his head, looked down at himself. "Ohhh, fuck." His kinked eyebrow said he suspected her.

It took five minutes or more, but he dragged himself upright and began to strip the ropes from her. Untied, she smiled up at him, straightened, unfolding her legs, not bothering to massage her wrists though they ached. Even standing, he was taller than her.

Then she reached out for his cock and tried to steer him back to the sofa.

"No. You think? Hell, no."

He pushed her down to the sofa, spread her legs with slaps to her inner thighs, then buried his face in her pussy and finger pumped her cunt. Two fingers, three? Four?

She came, arching, fingers tearing at the upholstery and cushion for he'd slapped her hands from his hair. She came with her ass lifted off the sofa, wrenching in air. He had a mouth to remember.

Then he spun her, facedown again. "You made this, and so…"

Parting her ass cheeks, pinning her down, he wet his cock on her arousal and slowly worked it into her asshole. "This time," he gasped. "It's going in all the fucking way."

With her still gathering air for essentials like staying alive, with the rush of her last orgasm pounding at her and his hand slipping around to massage her clit, she woke to a new stir.

Cock sliding into her ass. Squeezing in against the resistance of her body. Her mouth gaped.

The stretch was unnatural and infernal even for her. It hurt and pleasured her by strange ways that threw all of the sensations together.

And yet she wriggled back at him, encouraging him.

With his fingers on her and with that slow-pumping cock reaming her, with her desire for raw male possession, she found herself loving this.

Nothing mattered except that he was fucking her.

She clawed the sofa, crying out as another climax soared then blew apart her world. It blanked her mind and left her gasping with a wet cushion stuffed partway between her lips.

He pulsed inside her, groaning as he pulled out. Then he had her lie on the sofa and climbed over her to spoon with his back wedged against the sofa.

There would be come on the sofa and there was no ocean to wash everything clean. But it was his sofa. Not her concern. She wormed closer to his heated body, his muscles. The hard biceps draped over her neck made her feel safe and happy.

The TV had not stopped talking all the time they were screwing, and she wrinkled her brow.

How long did it talk for? Pictures of people killing each other seemed to take priority.

"You haven't shifted, yet." Wolfgang whispered. "Wait. I have something." He climbed over her and went to a room. His naked ass made her watch him walking. A door slammed then he returned.

A heart-shaped pendant hung from his hand as he climbed back onto the sofa and snuggled.

"Yours." He connected it at the back of her neck in a tight circle. Too small to fall off when she swam.

Then his hand moved down to wedge between her legs and fingers stroked her. She shut her eyes as sensations reawakened.

Again?

"Going to see if I can keep you edged. Stop your squirming."

Ahh. That. She wriggled but let him find her clit, sighing.

"Where is this necklace from? Not the other? The pearls were pretty."

"That one was to track you. This is because I want to give it to you, miss mermaid."

"Oh." She touched it as he touched her, then closed her eyes to feel how his fingers moved on her. She recalled the gold look to the necklace. "Do you keep many of these in your house?"

"Eh." He shrugged, breathed hard against her neck. "To be honest, it belonged to an old girlfriend. She returned it."

"You are a rich man to have such things. I was poor."

"Tell me," he said. "About your past. You never did."

"No more fucking?" Those fingers… playing. Already she

had ideas.

"Uh. No. Hell shall freeze over first."

Even so, how was she to speak when he did that?

"Talk. Or else I get out my flogger and nipple clamps."

What? Her eyes sprang wide open.

But she began to talk. "Eighteen twenty-nine was the year I was born. I think? Everything gets hazy after the first hundred years, and my mother was never sure of dates."

Dredging up memories from that long ago meant sifting through half-recalled images, words, glimpses of things that happened to her. She remembered the hurricane and spewed forth the entire scene. The day she died was engraved on her mind.

"They threw you overboard in the middle of a hurricane? Jesus." His body tensed. Even the muscles of the arm and hand he used to tease her halted in their mission and stiffened. He found her hand and clasped it, brought it higher so as to kiss her fingers.

"That's disgusting, terrifying," he said softly. "No words, I have no words to say what I want to about that. I'm sorry for you. For who you were."

And who she now was, she supposed. The hurricane was long ago, and she'd forgotten how it had scarred her. Those she preyed on usually spent their last moments in the throes of lovemaking. When she had been taken it was too brief, too thrown at her in the midst of a scene of pain, injury, and horror.

Then he added something in a puzzled voice that seemed pulled from somewhere else, from another realm of conversation. "You have no idea how different this is for me. To be like this."

Like what? He'd had girlfriends — he had said so. While she had really only had clients and prey. How could this be more different for him than it was for her?

She settled, however, and went on, delved further back to when she'd been a child in the slums of London, begging because her father was nonexistent in her life and her mother a laundress and wretchedly poor.

They exchanged questions, thoughts, and Wolfgang made comments that reminded her he was actually *listening* to her. No one, nobody had *ever* done this. Not even when she was human.

Only now did she realize how much of a hole there existed inside her. A person needed this. It was more life than blood. It was food for her soul. Some of her sadness seemed to fade away as they cuddled on the sofa in this human house with human things on the TV and this man wrapped around her.

What else might he teach her?

To her amusement, he kept on teasing her below. It did keep her on the edge, especially with him kissing her shoulder and neck.

After a long while, with shadows slanting over the pool outside and the light out there dulling, his fingers slipped away, hand slackening. He snored.

The change in her happened within a few minutes. She sensed it coming. Then… A wriggle in her body, a blur in the mind.

A rupture where everything *twisted.*

She had a tail again, but he was snoring. Smiling, she left him alone, waiting until her skin began to dry out before she nudged him awake with kisses on his nose and a slap of her tail on his feet.

"Oh." Bleary of eye, he sat up on his elbow then levered himself off the sofa.

Without doing much more, apart from wandering to another room and saying he had to get something from the 'fridge', he staggered up the stairs with her in his arms and took her to the pool.

She rolled then dived in, slipping through the water, her skin prickling with the coolness and breathing a sigh of its own as the liquid soothed it. A mermaid was meant for the sea.

Wolfgang kneeled and let the second fish plop from the bag into the pool. "You have completely screwed me." His slight smile said he didn't hold a grudge. "I'll make a date with you for tomorrow."

Standing slowly, stretching joints, he eyed her as she swallowed the very dead fish. It was cold, and she decided he must have kept it cool somehow. Another miracle of these times.

"I'll bring you some more tomorrow. Fresher." His head inclined. "Next time we do a cheese platter, antipasto, some wine. I'll make us a small banquet. I need to feed you. And to think I nearly shot you that day at the beach." He shook his head, scrubbed his hands through his dark, unruly hair.

Raffaela stared, and not only because of the ripple of muscles over his chest and stomach as he stretched, or the V lines of his belly ridges leading downward. No, not just those pretty parts of him. Idly, she flicked her tail to stay balanced.

On the beach, she'd never seen a weapon.

His words reminded her of how he had been. How brutal he had been. Had tiredness made him unguarded and let slip a fact he never meant to say?

When he headed for the stairs, his gait lurched a few times, and she remembered the shadows around his eyes.

Tomorrow, he would feed her more. This was good. She sank to the bottom, water gurgling about her ears, thinking. Perhaps she should urge him to go slower?

Had the experiment been all that he intended?

She had certainly learned something.

For once he neglected to turn out the lights inside the house and she watched him collapse on the sofa again, legs and arms sprawled out, and fall into another long, heavy slumber. Hours. The TV remained on. The night passed to midnight from the look of the moon and stars, and still he stayed there.

He had not eaten. Or drunk. Not since they had fucked.

Curious.

CHAPTER NINE

"You didn't bite me," were the first words he said to her on that tomorrow. It was mid-afternoon. "You could've have ripped out my carotid with those." He waved toward her, meaning her teeth, she presumed. "While I was asleep."

"True." Raffaela shrugged, knowing the movement would draw his eyes to her breasts as they rose and fell, seen then not-seen as water covered them.

There was a thrill to this. Pursuer and victim, but who was which? It was a game she had played for longer than he had lived. Never on land. That was new for her.

Who would come out on top?

Upon hearing the door open, then his steps, she'd swum to the shallower part of the pool, lying with her tail stretched behind her, the water sloshing from her swift passage. Her palms were flattened on the underwater ramp and her nipples played peekaboo.

His pants already showed signs of being tented by an erection. She smirked until he lifted his eyes.

"Why didn't you?"

"I was…" With her finger she drew circles in the surface of the water, spawning ripples. Her back felt the nudge of her hair where it drifted. "… as tired as you were, and you would not have been so careless as to leave your doors for me to open."

"*Huh.* Smarter than I thought. Yeah, the windows are locked down and the door locks are passworded." When she cocked her head, he read it correctly as puzzled and added, "Means you need the right combo of words tapped on a keyboard – written down – before it will unlock."

That seemed crazy. "Why? How?"

"I have things I want kept secret from people and things I don't want stolen." He'd turned to rummage in his brown bag. "As for how – it's complicated."

If he wanted to tie her up again, would she let him?

It seemed so unnecessary, considering.

"I could have killed you then broken out through a window," she mused.

His hand emerged holding a chain and a black dog collar.

"Nope. The glass is toughened."

And what was toughened glass? She could guess. There were so many new things, new words. Walking among humans once yearly had only let her see the surface of what mankind had invented and how people had changed.

He raised the tinkling chain, with his feet set apart and him watching her, as if he wished to see her response.

She was close enough to register the hazel-brown color of his eyes, the wrinkling around them, and a tiny scar on his forehead. Again, he wore a soft shirt that fit him perfectly. When he moved, she could see the heavy curves and ridges on his chest and stomach. At the end of his ill-shaped dove-gray pants his bare feet showed. They looked large when she thought of her own toes.

Men, she decided, had nice feet.

"Think of this as a compliment."

She looked up, pretending she had not been admiring his toes.

"No gag, No rope. Just this on your neck and the chain."

Oh. That was for her not a pet? Raffaela blew bubbles, letting her lower body drift while still holding onto the ramp.

"Why? Why should I let you collar me like a dog?"

"Because it pleases me and lets me control you still, just a little." He held up finger and thumb a fraction apart. "I like keeping control of my females."

"Females?"

That was not the proper way for a man to address his lovers. Even she knew this.

"Don't like that word?" He grinned maliciously. "How about my captive? Better? Because you are that."

He squatted down, played with the chain, looped it like a snake along the ground then up his leg, over his bent knee. Tempting her.

It did tempt her and was somehow seductive.

A chain and a collar.

For her. She imagined the man placing the collar on her neck, buckling it.

Making her his…

Desires ascended, whispering to her, washing away the centuries of loneliness. Her loneliness had been leeching away her soul. Nevertheless, she had survived, had been her own keeper, carer, and this, living in his pool, was surely fated to fail.

"Come, little captive." He twitched the chain.

With teeth denting her bottom lip, she contemplated Wolfgang, and thought idly about scaring him. No gun showed, anywhere. Was this a game or serious? When blood was involved calling it a game seemed wrong.

There had been and would be more blood. It was in the nature of her kind.

"Am I?" Asking was fraught with danger – the danger of encouraging something ever more forbidden. Chains and collars were for animal pets, not lovers. This was something her society, her time, would have considered unthinkable.

Memories surfaced of the day before, of their lovemaking. Her mind split between the past and the present. As if he had touched her, her intimate area pulsed with warmth.

Which was odd since she had nothing there until she shifted.

"You are my pretty captive, yes. I have you confined to my pool and at my disposal. The doors are locked to you." His head inclined. "You are argumentative, today. Come. Let's do some more research." He shook the chain, opened the collar. "Come to me."

That deceitful mouth of his smiled, as if he knew she would obey.

Raffalea swished her tail, languidly, pretending to think in spite of the burgeoning ache within. She prolonged the moment to tease him then swam over.

"Good. Thank you," he said as he removed the necklace, buckled the collar at the back, then rearranged it and clipped on the chain. She suffered the procedure, unmoving. "Up here."

After patting the very top of the ramp, where there was no water, he backed away. She shimmied up and lay with her head up and her lips parted.

As always, there was threat in showing her teeth. Before this, he had respected that.

Today?

With his foot, he casually flipped her onto her back and

stood on the chain beside her neck, as if victorious. Triumphant. She let him think it was so because she found she liked playing the victim with him.

Besides, one day she might need his mistakes.

Wolfgang looked down her body and sighed.

"Such beauty should never be left in the sea."

If that wasn't so flattering, she might have scoffed.

Having kneeled beside her, he trailed his fingers softly down her face, beginning at her hairline, going over her eyes and making her close them, over her nose, her lips. When he reached her mouth and delved in there in spite of her teeth, she was already aroused and squirming. Something about the way his foot pinned her and his casual dominion over her body did *things* to her. Nice things.

She left her lips parted. Though his hand moved lower and he kept his foot on the chain, his focus was on her face.

He watched her, watching him.

Awareness heightened but she saw only him. As she struggled with arousal, her breathing hitched.

When he reached her lower stomach, he stilled his hand, his relaxed fingers pointing downward like arrows aimed at her sex.

"Not turned on enough, yet?" he murmured. It was true that she had not shifted. "I have a fix. Something I was going to use anyway."

Wolfgang reached into a pocket in his pants, retrieved a small device then flicked at it with his thumb. It began to buzz.

"What is that—" she began as he pushed it onto her below, where everything was not yet human, where her female parts would appear after shifting. Her sex.

The buzz burrowed in, struck her an intimate and delicious blow, and made her arch into his hand.

Eyes locked on his, she stifled a moan. Her eyes rolled upward. Her hands clenched, her tail tensed, and—

Shift.

She came down to Earth, on her back, and breathing like a steam train. Above was sky. Blue sky.

Had she orgasmed?

In the middle of a shift? No. Couldn't have.

Certainly, she was panting uncontrollably. A wash of pleasure had ripped through and left her mind a jumble.

He was chuckling. "That worked."

"No. No," she found herself saying.

"No?"

She shook her head, gulped. The word had appeared without her assembling it.

"Come. You can walk."

He unfolded his legs and stood, pulled on the chain until she rolled over and found her feet, pushed herself upward to stand beside him, if a little wobbly.

"*Ahhh*, naked girl. Much better. I like having bits to play with."

After a brief kiss and fondle, with his hand clenching onto her butt – the fingers slipping partway into the split between each cheek – he headed for the steps. The chain was in his hand, so she followed.

The existence of her bare feet took a little while to get used. Her middle throbbed but she followed, one hand feeling at the collar, wondering why it felt so curious to wear one. The other necklace was gone, but she supposed wearing both at once would be a problem.

Although every so often he glanced back as if to see if she was still there, she could tell he was simply observing her body.

Which was entirely fine. She wore no clothes, and he was

male.

Now if he had been naked…

After he opened the glass door and they passed through, Wolfgang went deeper into the house with her in tow, moving away from the lounge room where they'd spent most of the previous day. Raffaela smiled.

She walked. Had feet. It was always a novelty, an adventure.

That she lived at all was something to celebrate. If not for Wolfgang's aborted revenge she would have killed herself.

"The kitchen." He gestured vaguely at the wall before them, which featured a long countertop with timber cupboards above and below, and a tall steel cupboard that hummed. There was a sink equipped with what she remembered were faucets. Those carried water. No pumping was needed. It simply poured out.

He turned to face her and leaned back against a cupboard, then tossed a towel to the floor before him.

"Kneel."

Then he simply waited, and she had to decide whether to obey. Obeying appealed to her, so she slowly kneeled, adjusting position until her knees did not hurt.

This was strangely sexual.

His erection was clearly poking at his pants, and she ran her tongue across her lips, teasing and eyeing him. More and more she had come to understand that simply by being before him, a siren was the ultimate temptation to man.

He had no chance of resisting her.

She did not need to sing. Or dance. Or be in the middle of the Ravening.

When this close, she only needed to *be*.

Even so, she thrust out her chest. It was fun to see his reaction.

He clucked his tongue. "Be good. I'm restraining myself. Today I have a plan to keep you on edge." Wolfgang's lips quirked. "And all without me having to touch you very much. You fucked with me yesterday but not today. I have your measure, as Shakespeare might say."

Shakespeare, she recalled, but he was still famous? Some things endured. And what was this about not having to touch her? It seemed an insult, though she could not say why.

Insults needed answering, and she knew how to reply.

Smiling, she raised her hands and cupped her breasts, feeling the weight of them before she slipped her thumbs over her nipples and revolving them softly, slowly. The brushing friction instantly stirred her. With her eyelids half-lowered, she concentrated on what she did.

"Why did I have to get a mermaid slut?" His gaze drifted lower, fixating on her female parts, pausing to watch her stimulate herself. "Fuck," he muttered, drawing in a long breath.

There was power in making him crave her. She raised her breast toward her mouth, sticking her tongue out as if to lick herself.

When almost there, with her tongue straining, he groaned.

He leaned over and grabbed her hair, twisting it, making her slide forward on her knees and the towel slid with her. He fumbled to yank down his pants and let his erection spring free. A drop of liquid glistened at the end.

With no further warning, Wolfgang dragged her even further, to shove her mouth to his cock. "Suck like your life depended on it. Which it fucking might."

Well then. Raffaela smirked. He'd probably felt her smiling against his cock.

She looked up, and while keeping rigid eye contact, slowly encompassed his cock's head with her mouth, opening wide, slicking over and licking down, stopping at the end of the cap-like head to let her tightened lips pop over and land on the shaft.

He cursed her quietly, perversely.

Then he roughly pushed her head onto himself, up then down again, making her take most of him in, then stopping dead and holding her in place when he slid to the back.

"Damn you." He stayed motionless, rigid, groin tilted forward. Stalled, with his dick jammed in her mouth, his fingers tangled painfully in her hair.

She inhaled through her nose.

For all of a long, few, violently quiet moments, she had him, owned him.

This was power.

She flicked her tongue over his shaft, around as far as it could reach, then circled back, while sucking, hard.

"Bitch, mermaid bitch." Gasping, Wolfgang met her eyes and the *look* in those was the very definition of foreboding. "What you get for tempting me…"

He popped from her mouth, slid out in a second, and hauled her to her feet by the chain.

She protested at the suddenness.

Spun around, she was hoisted partway onto the bench and before the metal sink, with her breasts over the edge hanging into the space of the sink… Poised there, forced to be still. She put her palms to the bottom of the sink.

He wrapped the chain of her leash around and around the faucets, then stepped back and sighed.

"Damn. What a fucking sight. Don't touch the chain, unless you want your hands tied, and a spanking. Or worse."

The threats were new. Should she speak? No.

She dearly wished to see what he would do next.

His pants went flying to the side. Reflected light from the

pool wrote slurred sunbeams on the walls, the white cupboards, on metal. His shadow loomed as he stepped in. He gripped one cheek of her ass, exposing her then pausing…

A moist stroke of his finger between her lips. One slick, tunneling exploration with that finger, a single pump then withdrawal…

He entered her with an abrupt slam.

Cock filled her from pussy to overwhelmed mind. Her mouth gaped.

God. She forgot to breathe.

Again he halted, fully deep, and he hissed through his teeth, then slammed in again. The thrust pushed her against the sink, and she grabbed the faucet so as not to headbutt it. Swearing, he yanked himself out. He paced behind her while she stayed there, tied by the neck, with her pussy pulsing rhythmically.

Wanting him.

At the spasm of her inner walls, she shut her eyes, licked her lips – remembering his taste and how his cock felt. She choked out a sound and squirmed her ass to the side. The underside of breasts lay against the sink's cold steel. Her nipples were pebble hard.

He paced again, slapped her ass once, stepped away. "I should jerk off on you. You deserve it." His hard fingers stroked down her spine and she squeaked.

"Please?" *That* was begging.

"You need me?"

She gulped. "Yes."

"No."

The chaos of desire had her, was tugging at her, making her need, making her want. The cramping of her pussy was close to painful.

And that one slap had woken small prickles of heat that only fed her lusts.

"Not coming yet. Neither of us. Hell, no." Wolfgang removed his shirt but retrieved and pulled on his pants.

After undoing the chain from the faucet, he tugged it and walked off. Again, she followed, naked, and with her lower parts feeling oddly squishy, wet.

He brought her to a bedroom, a room she recognized mainly from pictures on TV because the luxury was alien. The cleanness of these times when light was at their beckoning, windows were perfected glass, floors were not dirty, and walls were painted in fresh, bright hues.

Her mother's house had been, she admitted, a darkened hovel compared to likely any home within a thousand, thousand miles of this one. And yet humans seemed as flawed as ever and all they did was throw garbage in the sea and war on each other. The TV had showed that too.

They had also found new fetishes.

How rich was Wolfgang?

The right-hand wall, which she'd not at first noticed, was hung with whips and black leather masks, black-and-red harnesses, and other things she was certain were not meant for horses.

She tilted her head, somewhat overcome. And those other penis-like objects lined up on a shelf?

Dildos. Of course. *Some even had veins.* But they were the colors of the rainbow as well as the commoner color in here for such things – black.

"Lie down and stay there while I fill your holes with multi-cock." The amused tone gave way his intent – abusing her with something here. He pushed her shoulder while pulling on the chain leash, and she lay belly down on this bed with the crisp, shiny gray sheets that sat in the middle of the room.

Anything sexual would do her at the moment, and she knew he would eventually stick the real thing in her. She tempted him too much.

She shifted so her knees were on the floor and wriggled her bottom, still hoping.

Once he'd collected something from the wall, he dropped to the bed beside her then hauled her over his lap. She had to balance over him, hands on the floor and her toes on the other side of him, dug into the rug.

"First, I have to do this." He smacked his hand onto her butt, twice, then began to spank her harder, regularly, almost in time to the cadence of his words.

"I'm doing research on you." *Slam.* "And you try to mess with me?" *Smack.*

A startled squeak escaped her.

She had to admit it was an interesting way to punctuate his speech.

He had her yelping, squeaking, and even squealing, though every blow seemed calculated to hurt but not injure and when he stopped the hum of the burn sneaked between her legs. It radiated in an amazing way. His cock was hard too, for she felt it under her. She let go of his leg that she'd grabbed to steady herself.

She twisted her neck so she could look up at him.

"Stay," he repeated. "You'll want to hang on again for this."

As if to make it mandatory, he took one hand behind her back and pinned it there.

Another smack rained down. This one was *fire* — a broad, plank-hard slam from some object.

"You need to listen next time? Yes? This is a paddle. Should I stop?" But he added three more smacks with the paddle while she wriggled and tried to escape. "Stop moving or this continues."

Panting, she glared at him, sideways, and he wasn't letting her go.

"Will you obey, miss mermaid? No biting. No tempting me. No seducing unless I okay it?"

Or else more paddling? Little did he realize the aftereffects had her inner engine running even hotter. The pain had converted within, turned to a simmering heated mix that made her ache for more of him.

He couldn't tame a siren.

But she loved the play. The way he'd dragged her hand to her back. The narrow-eyed study of her that said he knew more than he said. Between them, there seemed an unspoken contract.

He knew she could still kill him. They both had their weapons.

She nodded, agreeing, submitting to this.

When he brought his hand low and offered it to her mouth, she licked the back, his knuckles, sucked on the tip of one finger, then drew the knuckle into her mouth and nibbled while they exchanged more looks. Seductive ones, of course.

His chuckle was low. He tasted of man, which – along with everything that had happened – made her let out a throaty sigh. There was pleading in that sound. How long would he make her wait?

"One more, for the blowjob on my fingers." Then he drew back his paddle, high, and gave her one last stinging smack that felt as if it should rattle her teeth.

A moment of stillness, before the paddle clattered to the floor and he plunged fingers into her cunt and kept them there. She arched as much as was allowed by her position and by her hand being stuck behind her.

His fingers wriggled.

"Ffffuck," she whispered. She didn't swear often, but this…

"Good mermaid. Now, this." The fingers withdrew and something large was thrust into her where they had been. It was left in place, stretching her. The placing of it inside had somehow also jammed a different and softer prong onto her clit region.

She frowned, kneading the floor then grasping his leg. He still had her wrist.

"What is that?"

"A vibrating dildo, of sorts. This too." He probed her asshole with some pre-lubricated thing, wormed it inside. It was smaller than the other, for which she was grateful.

Then she heard a soft click, two, and the dildos burst into lustful song, playing with her down there, buzzing. Rendered speechless, she bent her back striving to get more then less then more as her body found the strange vibrations painfully arousing, until—

Bliss. The explosion of a climax rammed through her and held her in thrall.

Shuddering, oblivious for those nirvanic seconds, she discovered she was moaning and still held over his lap, and she was staring at the floor.

These devices were demonic.

He dumped her off his lap into a kneeling position, though at first she had to hold the side of the bed or risk collapse. Ignoring her state, he dressed her in a harness, snugged things down, buckling, tightening, wedging those dildo things inside her ever deeper. The straps went around and under her breasts, tucked between her legs, went around her waist.

And there were metal bits here and there dangling from

it.

"Am I a horse?" she said, straightening, but still on her knees.

"There." He patted her butt. "A mermaid pet horse? Maybe?" Wolfgang snorted.

His eyes glinted when he pulled her to her feet, and his voice was low and dedicated. "A leathered-up girl with butt plug and cunt plug?" He rubbed his shadowed chin then tucked back a swathe of his black hair that had fallen over his eye.

The chain and collar were employed again as he led her over to the sofa. He cleared his throat, walking ahead of her nonchalantly, but she'd seen his dick. That erection must be bothering him.

Raffaela smiled, wishing she could do what she used to when she lived on the streets – take a bet on what he'd do with it.

"Those things I stuck in you, I can press a button on this remote." He showed another rectangle like the one that turned on the TV. "And it will switch on."

He pressed. She squeaked and folded over in shock at that invading buzz on her clit, and… the others inside her.

"So"—he swung around, walking backward for a few steps until his legs hit the back of the nearest sofa—"So… Fuck me, a leathered-up girl slash mermaid. Right. I can keep you shifted, aroused…" He swallowed, Adam's apple bobbing as he again rubbed at his mouth, jaw. "And hopefully walking about."

He stalked toward her, suddenly determined, grabbed her arm and hustled her to the pool wall, pushed her to it face-first, took both her hands and raised them high, pinned them, wrists together above her head. Using one hand, he slipped off his pants then kicked them aside.

He extracted the small plug from her ass, tossed it away then levered the nearest straps aside or undid them. Something akin to a growl left his throat. "How can I resist? You walking about in this? Tits sticking out, ass like a ripe peach… Stay."

He kissed her hair, her ear, bit her neck. From the corner of her eye, she saw him hold up the remote and press it. She braced herself.

Not as big a buzz, and a little uncomfortable but it set her to thinking sex, made her press backward as his cock pushed in, sliding into her ass, making it feel overfull and on the verge of too much, too soon. She hissed at the odd tweak of pain as he took her, solidly thrusting.

But the thing on her clit kept buzzing at her. Between the two of them – man and thing, and the dildo stuffed inside her pussy…

She was soon teetering on the edge of another climax and he was grunting as he went in, pinning her hands so firmly onto the glass that it squeaked as her palms slid.

The dildos fucked her, filled her *everywhere*, while he pushed in, and the buzz climbed, strengthened. There was another thrust, another, countless more with her tensing, trembling, her body confused as to what was in her where.

The world spun, throbbed, her legs shook.

Pinned to the glass, penetrated and filled, she came and came, and felt him fuck her a few more times before he also climaxed. His come was heated, and with the push of a last, solid thrust, he stilled, his weight on her back, his fingers kneading her wrists.

The device kept molesting her.

Too much.

Rent mindless, mouth open, she spasmed into a final climax, her lower body jerking against the cold glass.

"Damn." He pressed his head to hers, his muscled-up body enfolding her.

The buzzing finally stopped. Her clit was numb. And when he slid his cock from her, she was left to slide down the glass to her knees.

* * * * *

The day was spent in various ways — watching him prepare a meal using the wondrous machines in his house, a meal he fed to her while she kneeled before him. And it was spent being experimented on by various settings on the devices, as well as being screwed twice more — on the bed and over the dining room table.

She asked him about the institute. The scientists studied the sea and the animals in it. Not her type though, because she did not exist. He'd smiled at that.

By the end of the day he'd fed her far more than he had eaten and made love to her more than she thought he'd intended to. His enthusiasm for pacing himself and not fucking her had been trampled by his need to actually do things to her.

Which was fine, in her humble opinion.

Before he returned her to the pool in the late afternoon, he dressed her in a long silken gown with laces down the back then had her pirouette before him.

"You look so beautiful."

Raffaela smoothed her hand down the front, dabbled her fingers over the tiny cloth-covered buttons. "It is pretty." She had never owned anything like this. All the possessions she had ever owned could have been carried in a single large suitcase. She'd not even owned a dog, unless you counted a mongrel that had followed her. Like her, it had sought food, a safe place to be, a safe companion.

So why did she want to become a human again?

Success was not guaranteed. Riches were not. Safety was not.

He took up the leash he'd released her from earlier and reattached it. "Back to the pool. You can take it off up there."

A thought occurred as she trailed after him. "A girlfriend owned this?"

"Yes. Good guess."

"You've had a lot of them? Had sex with them?"

"Yes. And yes."

"But married none?"

"No."

Clearly marriage and morality were as messy as in her times, only maybe worse? Men would screw her in alleys but never tell their wives. Now it seemed they had a lot of girlfriends and never married any.

She recalled the other thing she'd meant to say. "Do not forget to eat. You didn't last night."

At the glass door Wolfgang stopped and turned, put his back to the door then reeled her in using the chain. He tucked his hand and the gathered chain under her chin.

"You watched me?"

She nodded.

"I will. You know…" A line formed between his eyes. "I almost wish I'd never had the other girls."

"Girls? Women?"

"They were women, but I like to call you all girls." His kiss was tender. A press on her lips then he withdrew and eyed her.

"Why?" she murmured.

His grin was devilish. "It makes you mine, more than

woman does. Like this does." The leash tightened at her neck. "Because I get to do this." As he'd said the words, his hand dragged the dress upward and slipped beneath to toy between her legs.

"Hmmm." She closed her eyes and let her legs relax to allow his hand to touch her. "I do like that. But you must eat."

"I will." He let the dress fall, turned to the door and twisted the handle. "Thank you. I'm… glad you said that."

Glad?

All of her fatigue, her bruises, the vague aches in her intimate parts, those vanished when she shifted, but Wolfgang did not have that advantage. So, of course he must eat.

That night, she watched him through the pool glass again, idly flicking her tail. He did eat, but not very much as far as she could judge. It made her feel sad, for some reason.

Because I'm addicting him to me? Or am I getting addicted to him?

Not just that. She was growing to like him.

This could never last. It would end. That was why there was sadness.

The Ravening would come, and what would he do then?

Through a slim gap at the side of the cloth that concealed the pool, she looked out at the ocean. It was dark but eventually the moon rose. She kept her eyes glued on the slit, hoping for – no, pining for – a glimpse of the sea.

In the painted glow of moonlight, as waves washed in with a distant booming and roaring, summoning her, she saw something that made her chest thump.

There. A tail larger than would be found on any fish venturing into the shallows. And no dorsal fin. For a microsecond, she saw the pale face of a man. *A male, not a man.*

She backed away from the glass, frightened. No merfolk had ever been friendly. None she had approached anyway.

They also could not reach her.

They could not, would not, rescue her anyway, even if they knew she was here.

CHAPTER TEN

Their debauched relationship continued for days that stretched into what she added up to being a week. Wolfgang declared a need to study her, and yet the research never progressed much beyond them making love many times each day. His experiment seemed to be going nowhere. To walk about his house was not of any practical purpose, except when it came to fucking.

He ate less than a man of his size should, she was certain of this.

He grew thinner in the face, more haunted looking. Shadows painted his eye sockets. Whereas she stayed the same. Each night she transformed into her mermaid form and her wounds and bruises healed.

Though the vast loneliness of the ocean had been banished, it was replaced by a strained waiting, of wanting more than this isolated dedication to sex.

Yes, Wolfgang told her about his life, about science, measuring pollution, and studying the levels of tiny pieces of garbage in the sea. He even told her about dissecting fish and other sea creatures so as to do his marine research, but it seemed as if he kept some details away from her, as if he hid things. Why would he do this?

Raffaela knew little of how to interact with men or humans, or nothing recent. Secrets, he had those. And she? She had only one.

She had said everything he wanted to hear, even the name of the last man she'd pulled under, made love to, and drowned. *Merrick.* She regretted that; it would only have brought him sorrow.

The Ravening was coming, but they had many weeks before it was due.

Once it came, once it scratched at her with those hungry claws, she would warn Wolfgang. Then? He would either release her or kill her, or she would end up killing him. That was her secret. It was one he might figure out on his own.

A secret that was not a secret.

Sadness was coming, abysmal sadness, but now was now. A mermaid was made for the present and not the future. She made no diaries, no photographs, no true memories for him. That she did not appear in his images shook him. Though she'd never seen a photograph made as he made them with his cellphone, she understood.

For something to be a solid part of his world, an absolute fact, and yet fail to work, it would be a shock. It was a little bit like being thrown into the sea because people thought you bad luck? How callous, and how complete a denial of her very existence that had been.

The shock had never left her.

Anyway, she could do nothing.

And so, she shoved her forebodings aside.

The fucking was fun. The things he made her do…

Even the aches, the bruises, the pains.

Today – she looked down at her breasts – was a day for

clamping things to her nipples.

The first shiny clamp was already biting at one of them. The chain joining it to another clamp swung as he leaned in from his kneeling position to ready her for the second.

"Such a good mermaid."

Her mouth was an *O*, as she absorbed the throb and spike of pain and the susurration of pleasure from where he sucked at her other nipple. To make it perky, Wolfgang had said. She thought it was already perfectly perky and upstanding.

He raised his head and pulled his mouth off her, sucking as he did so.

She hissed, inhaled, eyes shuttering.

Now it was wet *and* perky.

His large finger and thumb slipped on the nipple as he pinched at it… as the opened clamp approached.

"Owie," she whispered, pushing her chest forward because he'd tugged at her. He opened the clamp wider.

It bit down and she squealed, then smiled at the look of the silver-toned decorations. They hurt but also emphasized a very sexual part of her.

"Siren," she added, softly, correcting him.

"What was that?" He edged up onto the sofa that was behind him, then hooked her collar with one finger, urging her to join him on his lap. There, his cock awaited her. It was even perkier than her tits.

"Siren is a better word. Don't you think?"

He pulled her over him, adjusted her spread-eagled position, and made her sit while he squeezed his cock slowly inside her.

"Why?" His smile was strained as he did the first small thrust then pumped out and in again, found the chain connecting the clamps and put downward pressure on them.

She watched, open mouthed, fascinated, as always, by the feel of the man entering her, by the look of herself impaled. She felt for where his cock disappeared into her entrance and her fingers slipped along her lips to either side of his member. He halted. Seconds passed, agonizing seconds. Then he grabbed at her to hold her still with rigid fingers, tilted his hips abruptly, and she gasped, enraptured, as he slid higher inside her.

"Oh. God." That stretch… his evil chuckle.

"Why siren?"

"Oh. Oh. *Ummm.* Because. You're addicted to me, can't stop. Can you?" She let her head rock back, blissfully absorbed in what he was doing, what his cock was doing, while his hands moved up to hold her tits and haul on the chain. She was enslaved to the bite of that metal, to the push of his cock.

Wolfgang grunted. "I need to fucking gag you."

"Truth. What I said." She glared.

Which only prompted him to stick much of his hand into her mouth to stop her talking, as much as he could fit while he fucked her on his lap, then he turned her to plow her over the end of the sofa, with the clamps doing horribly bad, and nice, and painful things, all at once. It messed with her head, made her come with such delicious intensity.

She had gnawed his fingers, when they'd arrived in her mouth, slobbered on them, had gained a modicum of revenge.

Though that did result in him whipping her ass later, then fucking it hard.

That, in her opinion, only underlined the truth in her statement.

All part of the game. The sadistic, orgasmic mind game.

Except she had riled him a little. The gleam in his eyes

when she'd said that *truth* – it betrayed a certain realization.

He knew.

He was addicted and had no clue as to how to extricate himself.

Neither did she.

Weeks passed.

Weeks of them madly screwing with his sadism running slightly amok. He teased her, flogged her, spanked her, and yet he held back some part of himself.

The number of times he said, "You're different, so different from the others," was only surpassed by her telling him to feed himself. He had been remembering to eat more than those first days, but it worried her. Killing men with sex was in her nature during the Ravening. Apparently, watching a man starve himself triggered some maternal instinct she never knew she owned.

How could she *not* be different from his human girlfriends was more to the point. What did he mean by that?"

However, the snuggling, the cuddles that happened more and more were a surprise.

Both of them liked it. Since he instigated them, he must like it.

He even told her about Merrick. Initially, he'd employed the man as a full-time gardener of the house and property, and they had become friends then lovers. Merrick had moved into the house. Telling her about the man she had taken from him seemed the ultimate in trust and forgiveness.

Snuggling though.

Snuggling was more than pleasant or a matter of trust. It meant him gently brushing his fingers through her hair to untangle it. His leg over hers with his toes prodding at her calves. His weight on her, yet so peaceful, not like at other times. His warm breath on her neck.

This overwhelmed her.

Filled her with something amazing, a glorious joyousness. A quiet soft joy.

It was novel, the same as she had never tasted caviar or worn gold jewelry, never ever had she been kissed awake when she fell asleep beside a man. Never played a video game, or drunk champagne.

Snuggling was new and enchanting.

He loved enfolding her in his arms while they lay on the sofa or bed, with a movie running on the TV or Beethoven playing. A few times it was Shakespeare – Wolfgang had decided her education on the arts was abysmal.

A few times, tears had sneaked from her eyes and silently lipped the lids, to wander off and trickle down her face.

And every night she would watch him sleep from underwater in the pool.

When did *like* progress to something greater?

She did not know and wished it never would. Or hadn't. She knew nothing of love.

Her loneliness had been bad enough without memories of something… better.

The Ravening was not on her but the twinges of it poked her, beckoning her with bloody, come-soaked fingers. It was in her nature. And, after all, death might be the best answer for her.

She'd been going to anyway.

Each night he slept sprawled out, probably snoring, and sometimes with his eyelids flickering as if he dreamed. She pressed her face to the glass of the pool and watched. The swirls of water made him seem unattainable and a being from another mystical world.

The twinges grew, despite her knowledge of what was normal. It should not be here.

Not yet. It was too soon.

Perhaps her separation from the ocean had effects she knew nothing of?

The twinges strengthened.

And so the night came when she begged him. "It's time. You must let me go."

They lay on a blanket on the grass beside the pool. The grass strip was only along one side but the soil beneath was soft. There had been rain the day before.

She wasn't facing him, and she had said it quietly, because she had to tell him but hated what it meant.

This was a starry night, one where all the twinkling above surpassed any sky in her memory. She wore a little, frothy pink dress and was praying she would not shift.

"Low pollution tonight and no clouds," Wolfgang told her, caressing her hair. "The reason for the stars being bright."

"Oh. I see."

She breathed in. "Did you hear what I said?"

"I did. The answer is no, Raffaela." He lifted his head.

She was nestled into his shoulder and chest, and his arm lay across her. He brought his hand up to angle her head a little toward him, until their eyes met, a gentle meeting as she gazed up at him.

By now, she trusted him enough not to be alarmed by the denial. Besides, he could do nothing to her that she would not do to herself.

"If you don't, I fear I will kill you. The Ravening comes."

"How soon?" His brow creased.

"I cannot be sure, but I can feel it. Here." She laid her hand over her heart then on her stomach. "We both know your experiments only let me walk about in your house. Though I do enjoy the effects, I cannot go elsewhere."

He said nothing.

"Wolfgang."

"I will not release you."

"But if you do not—"

"I won't fucking do it," he snarled. Then he shut his eyes, swallowed. "I can't."

"Release me, please. I will come back to you."

"I can't! You're right. I am addicted to you. This is all so wrong." His voice dropped in tone, became a ragged whisper. "How can I keep you when I'm fucking myself to death?" He laughed. "Stupid."

She found his hand, fondled it. What was the answer?

"How can you ever walk among men? You'd draw them. They'd die in your flames like dumb moths."

"Wet mermaid flames?" she said, teasing him but also forlorn.

"Yeah. Those. I have thought on this. There is another possibility, though I should get your consent before I try it."

She pulled away from him, turned over. "What is this?"

"A brain probe. If, by surgery, a probe were to be implanted, we could trickle small amounts of electricity into you…"

Her mouth had fallen open.

"They do it to stop seizures. Pick the right spot and it should cause arousal, which… Okay. I can see it's a no, for now." He searched her face.

"It is a no. As in forever a no."

"Hmmm." He flopped onto his back. "Let's look at the stars awhile. Instead of me talking brain surgery."

If she hadn't thought him serious…

A breeze whistled across her ears and stirred his hair. A night bird made strange sounds from the line of pine trees that shielded the front of his property. And the sea, the sea murmured to her, calling her. The smell of salt and fish never left the air.

Raffaela held up her hands and stared at how they blocked the stars. She felt the suck and surging pull of the ocean that she had refused to acknowledge. It had always been there but had been less palpable. Now, it tugged at every fragment of her body. The ocean knew she was never gone, that she belonged in the depths and chasms, in the frolicking waves, and it was calling her home.

The sea was in her blood. She could not survive for much longer without swimming in the waters that were a true part of the immensity of the ocean.

Hence, the Ravening came early.

"I am sorry. My solution is a bad one." He rolled over to put his hand on her breast and ran his thumb over her through the light dress. "Stay with me. Don't shift. Be my girl a little longer."

"Mmm." She sighed and snuggled into him again, toying with his shirt buttons. He wasn't simply meaning tonight. "I will."

"You see, I love you. I'm fairly sure of it. This is new for me."

Oh. Fuck. And new for her.

She closed her eyes. *No.*

Yes.

But also no, no, no.

What was she to do?

"The thing is, I've been a bad man. A very, bad man. I don't deserve you."

"Shhh." She placed her forefinger over his mouth, felt him kiss it. "You're not that bad. You cannot be. I've lost count of how many men I have drowned. A thousand or more." Bitten to death, allowed to bleed out. Whose life force she had taken.

"Then we are both bad, and I am lost. I don't think I can survive without you."

"Wolfgang, I don't know what to do," she whispered. "What to say."

"Say nothing except this. Do you love me?"

She considered the bright, bright stars. "I don't know if a mermaid can love."

She was pretty sure she was lying. Fairly sure she had indeed fallen in love.

But she was even more sure the Ravening was closer than she had imagined.

Maybe it was his declaration of love that had triggered this increase in her *need*. Her mouth twisted. She could push it down for now, but soon it would be too strong.

"Tell me," she said to distract herself. "What did you do that was so wrong?"

"I cannot say. I will not. But it was terrible. I lost sight of my humanity. Not sure I ever had any."

She shook her head in disbelief.

"Sometimes…" Wolfgang lifted her hand and pretended to count her fingers, pressing each one upward, stroking them. "I think you may be more human than I am."

* * * * *

The next morning she found herself sleeping on the bottom of the pool, with a wicked hunger inside her. On the tiles above, she heard the slap of feet.

He was here.

She stiffened, swirled in a circle, then sped to the surface, flinging a spume of water high.

She showed her teeth.

"You need to go, *now!*"

"What?" He stopped at the top of the steps. "What do you mean?"

The water gurgled at her ears.

She smelled him. This was not the smell of an available male; it was the smell of life.

Cautiously he came closer, halting a few yards from the pool's edge.

"Is it the Ravening?"

Though she was not mindless, the craving was too strong. She lunged, skating and sliding across the shallow water on the ramp, launching herself with a flick of her tail muscles. He spun and fled down the steps. The door slammed.

She hadn't come close to getting him, had not used her siren song.

Raffaela lowered her head to the concrete and shut her eyes.

Next time she would be compelled to sing.

The Ravening had come.

She needed blood and death, and a life to eat.

CHAPTER ELEVEN

Wolfgang leaned his shoulder on the door. Not to keep it shut – to steady himself. The side of his face was on the cool glass, and his heart was thudding at him, reminding him of how he had moved down those stairs. She'd almost grabbed him.

He'd run like a fucking banshee batshit suicide machine. He laughed at himself, wiped at his eyes with finger and thumb.

To get away from her – his love, his mermaid with the pointy fucking teeth, he'd run.

"Raffaela…" he murmured as he side-eyed the top of the stairs, wondering if she would appear there, snarling.

When she didn't, after another minute or so he heaved himself upright and wiped his mouth.

"Think, fool."

What could he do? The Ravening did not answer to logic or science, that was obvious.

She needed to eat a human? Regular takeout wouldn't help him here.

Because he needed to see her and to be certain she had not found some miraculous way to escape, he went to the sofa and lowered himself.

Raffaela waited for him, staring through the glass barrier that was all that stopped her from killing him. Her tail silently stirred, puffing up sand.

Her siren song should, theoretically, not reach him through the glass. It was soundproof. On the other hand, the Ravening was not science. None of this was based on factual evidence.

If he went out there again, for whatever reason, he should be as prepared as he could be.

There was only one solution to this. Two, if you counted letting her go back to the ocean.

His real solution: Find her someone she could eat.

Using her tail to stay at eye level, she bobbed in the water. The sunlight reached down through the water and cast serpentine ripples across her tail, her back, her side. It made her scintillate like a living jewel, and when she turned full circle in the water, rolling her body, the light played across her front.

She was teasing him with those. Tits. Breasts. He'd kissed those, could feel them under his hands, in his mouth.

He laughed. A fucking obvious tease that had made his dick hard in seconds.

"You want a human? I'll find you one."

Nothing was impossible. The latest philosophy? *You can do anything you put your mind to.*

The nearest town was more of a village that filled seasonally with tourists but drive past it to the next place and you found a city. Merrick knew, had known, the ins and out of the drug trade, of where the dealers hung out, who to buy from.

It was recreational for the two of them, him and Merrick – only nightclubs, not dirty alleys or looking to get a hit in the worst neighborhoods, but he knew where was good.

Knew where to look for the down and outs, for those on an OD path, those who would not be missed if they disappeared.

He went looking for them, found one the third night he tried, under a bridge, which was classic. The man was all by himself – sprawled out wearing a stench-laden coat with pee on his pants, grass in his dank fair hair. Wolfgang hauled him into the trunk and drove off, having checked to be sure there was no CCTV or anyone observing him.

He drove off with a man in his trunk – still breathing but so shallowly he was as good as dead.

When he closed the garage door – having waited for the slam and for the outside to be gone, until it was just him and this trunk with a victim in it – when he opened it, the man was goddamned dead.

"Well. Took care of that part. Now I don't feel so guilty." He shrugged then grabbed hold of the canvas he'd lined the trunk with. There was always a plus to everything, they said. "Wait…" he shook his finger at the guy. "Wheelbarrow."

Dumping an entire clothed body in his pool seemed almost sacrilegious, as if this was some rite of sacrifice.

Though undressing the fucker was gross. He did it, however, there in the lit-up garage, with the fluorescent lighting adding a certain crime-scene noir to the dark deed. He undressed the guy, bundled up the clothes, decided those could go in a garbage can somewhere miles away. Then he wheelbarrowed him down the outside of the house, hosed him off, 'cause grossness…

Then he dressed in his patented siren-protective gear. Headphones with sound-deadening qualities. Bike helmet.

Nose plugs — because who knew what they did to a man, really? Besides the guy still smelled.

Then he went up the little used side steps to the pool, unlocked the gate there, and dumped the body on the grass strip, and ran. Wolfgang was pretty certain she'd been singing to him — she'd been sat up half-out of the pool with her mouth wide open.

His gut had also done a weird flutter as if, somehow, she had affected him.

"Mission accomplished. Surely?" Though he would have some cleaning up to do after.

His pool filter would die in the face of trying to filter out flesh and intestines and god knew what else.

So he switched it off until she did the deed and ate him. He wandered to the pool wall.

Raffaela was swimming at the bottom of the pool eyeing him as if he were a steak sandwich and a bucket of nuggets all in one.

"Fuck." He ran a hand through his hair. After all that? This would work, wouldn't it?

No. it did not.

A few hours later, he dressed in the protective gear again and hastily hooked the guy with a rake. He pulled the smelly corpse through the side gate, then buried the guy on the property in one of the garden plots Merrick had dug.

Hand on heart, he said a few lame words over the grave. *Ashes to ashes, dust to dust, you fucker, now I have to do this again.*

Like that.

She had not lunged at Wolfgang, and from the mythology he recalled, maybe sirens relied on men going to them most of the time? Even so, his heart was about to lodge a protest over all the scares.

Dead did not cut it. He needed *alive*. More alive than that one anyway.

He had another idea. Back to the city he went. Same car but with more cash in his wallet. Bait.

Slowly he drove into the suburb he aimed for, avoiding the obvious traffic lights and main streets where CCTV might catch him. This was where the deals went down, according to Merrick who had lived here years ago.

His hunting ground, now.

He cruised, looking for the right person. This was not going to be as easy as hauling away a mostly dead guy.

Another three nights and he found a promising human. Very alive but possibly wounded.

There'd been a *pop-pop* of gunfire but fairly muted, low velocity or something, only one scream and he'd seen her drop something a man scooped up and ran away with. No police sirens, yet.

Rain drizzled onto the windshield and his wiper blades shooshed up and down. He parked, switched off the engine, opened the door and exited, brought the collar of his black coat up higher, settled his fake glasses into place.

Streetlights reflected in opalescent rainbows off the puddles.

There.

Wolfgang headed toward the alley where the woman had fled. Dressed in jeans and jacket, she looked more like a dealer than a hooker.

The gun was in his coat pocket.

"You okay in there?" he asked, quietly. "Did I see someone shoot you? Need a hand? The cops?"

"No cops."

"No? Hospital? Emergency? I can drive you?"

"I can—" She coughed and in the dull light he thought he saw blood on the ground. Lungs then. Maybe.

"If you have a chest wound, we need to hurry."

He could barely see her, leaning up against the brickwork – mostly her eyes gleamed.

"Not going to call anyone?"

"Not… tonight."

He thought she was chewing her lip.

"Okay. You look decent, man. Don't try and fuck me over. I got no money or nothin' on me anymore. He got all that."

"Sure." Wolfgang stepped away. "My car is this way."

He led the way, heard her follow. There'd be blood on the seat, so he'd need to clean that up. He'd stop in a street he knew, in a dark spot where the lights were out, pull the gun on her, zip tie her wrists, put her in the trunk.

"I've been doing naughty things tonight, myself," he tossed that back at her, laughed. "I'm going a back route to miss the CCTVs. That okay? If not, maybe we will just call for an ambulance?"

"It's fine." She stopped to cough again. "Keep fuckin' going. And hey, thanks."

"No problem. Karma comes around, goes around."

If this was love, if this was romance, it was a very effed-up romance.

It wasn't quite the same, he discovered, catching a living and conscious person. Especially one who was coughing and bleeding all over your car.

By the time he reached the house she was almost done for, but not quite. Getting her into the trunk had been easier. She'd been mobile but weakening fast from shock. He drove fast.

When the garage door was shut, he popped the trunk to find she'd sprayed copious amounts of blood everywhere. He'd have to scrub his car for a year to get it all out. Her breathing was shallow, bubbly. And he needed her alive. He pulled her and the canvas out, took off her jacket, the shoes, the jeans, then he stopped. Her lips looked bluish, and she barely reacted to anything he did.

Such a pretty woman too. Crewcut black hair, black nails, studs in her ears, her nose, and probably her nipples from the bumps in her shirt. So many tattoos, so many gorgeous tattoos.

He shook himself out of the appraisal.

Throwing her in with the rest of her clothes on would have to do. If he tried to undress her, she might die before Raffaela reached her. Wolfgang bundled her into the wheelbarrow and took off down the side path, hauled her up the side steps.

Still alive. Still alive. She'd rolled her eyes toward him. Thank god.

Quickly, he donned his gear, and tossed her into the pool enclosure. Then did the usual slam-shut, lock, and run.

Different. This time was different. He heard dragging noises, a shriek, then splashing.

By the time he was inside the house and had run up to the pool wall, the woman was in the pool.

The water was decorated with intertwining spirals and puffs of blood. He didn't shift from his spot. The kissing, the nakedness — as Raffaela slowly stripped off the rest of the clothes — the downright eroticism as the stranger died in ecstasy with his mermaid's mouth on her below.

God.

Shaken, he stepped away and could not look at the very last of it.

That would be engraved on his brain.

Once he had gathered his wits, Wolfgang trailed back up the steps, boots splashing in the water spilling down them.

At the top, mouth agape, he observed that a small hurricane had hit the pool area. Water was everywhere, the white seat was overturned, as was the table. Feet balanced at the pool's edge, he looked into the depths. Raff stared up at him from below, eyes wide and green. The water roiled with pinkish hues and the woman lolled about down there also, clearly dead, leaking only small amounts of deeper red. He fished out the clothes with the pole, left them in a sodden heap.

This could not go on.

He could not keep doing this – which was a shock to him, as he'd always thought himself practical.

Merrick would've aced this.

He shut that down.

No more fucking thinking about Merrick. His temples were aching from the loss he knew he must suffer.

"Come!" he croaked, beckoning, then said it louder, "Come!"

She swam underwater, body wavering from the refractions of light, and surfaced to lock her arms over the edge. Without saying more he walked to the ramp and she followed. Kneeling there brought her even closer, close enough to cup her face in his hand.

"I have to let you go, my mermaid. Do you understand? I cannot keep on doing this. Thought I could but… I can't."

She nodded in his hand, laid her face to the side and rubbed against him, her brow furrowed.

"Now. It has to be now while I am strong."

He scooped her up, with difficulty. Her tail made balancing her weight awkward. Most of the times when he'd carried her, she'd been shifted.

He did not dare to make her shift. It would devastate him, he thought, to see her again as a woman, and he might stop dead and falter.

"It's best for you." He maneuvered down the side steps with his wet, heavy, very sad-looking girl. "I'm sorry."

"Don't be. It's best for you too. I can see that. I remember human things. I've made you murder someone. Sort of?"

He grunted at that, refusing to follow her down that path, down into his past actions. Fuck today.

The sand sank under him, shells dug into the soles of his feet. The soft crunching made by his passage across the beach to where waves ebbed and flowed reminded him of far better days. He'd spent so much time here. So much wonderful time.

Today was overcast, grey and dismal, and appropriate for this ending.

He must let her go.

But what if.

What if he only…

All the possibilities railed at him, and none of them were both kind to her and right, or even good science. To hope to be made into her species, a merman, and what an odd word *merman* was, it was his best dream. Such a strange hope.

To be lost in the ocean with her, forever, exploring the deep trenches, chasing fish, seeing things no human could ever quite see in the same way… It would be glorious. And yet, one thousand or more men she had drowned. None had become merfolk. A vital ingredient was missing. Why her? Why had she changed?

There should be an answer.

He did not know it and had no one to question. So, this was what he must do.

"You must never return, Raffaela. Never. I would keep you forever if I could. I would not ever let you go again. It's who I am. Weak, if pushed." He smiled wanly. How well he knew the truth of that.

She nodded, brow and mouth pinched.

Wolfgang waded out until waist-deep then lowered her into the water, only to find her arms locked about his neck.

"My love," she whispered.

My love – an arrow to the heart. Painfully so.

He should've strangled Cupid.

She kissed him, and he sighed, returned the kiss for long enough to feel a stir.

Then he broke away. "No. Don't do this. If you shift… if you do, I may forget what I decided. That would not be good."

"No. I guess not." Her mouth twisted in regret. "I will never forget you, my Wolfgang."

"Nor I you, my precious girl. You woke a part of me I thought long-dead – my heart."

"Is that a line from a play? Romeo and Juliet?"

"No. But it should be."

"Write one for me." She pawed his dampening shirt – the sea was climbing up the cloth – put her nose to him and inhaled. Her lips trembled. Then she met his eyes. Already the ocean tugged at her hair, fanning it out into languorous scarlet curls.

Sadness passed across her irises, fashioned by the wavering reflections of sea and rising sun.

Gently, he pulled her arms from him, released her, then moved away. "Go, my love."

He'd never said *my love* to anyone. Because I'm a bastard, he reminded himself.

"Goodbye," she whispered then turned and did a shallow dive. With a strong push and swirl of tail, she dived deeper, and was gone. Only her shadow was left, flitting in the dull gray-blue sea, heading outward until it too vanished.

He blew a last kiss into the wind. "Find the edge of the world for me, find dragons and whales, pet the seals in Antarctica. Swaying palms, coral reefs. Everything I cannot see."

His imagination went elsewhere for a while as he stood there, pants soaked, waves shushing against him.

This was the hardest thing he had ever done, and that was saying something. Such suffering and pain he had, once upon a time, seen and caused, and yet this was the hardest ever.

"Pussy," he muttered. "Fucking pussy."

Eventually, he returned to the house, walked up the beach, dripping. He sat down in the sand, with his back against the concrete below the pool wall and stared out to sea for a bit longer.

Regrets, he had more than a few.

An hour, two, passed by. All his recriminations and regrets wound down to nothing.

He shoved himself to his feet, brushed off the sand and nodded at the ocean, to her. "I never deserved you. Always that was true. But I guess trying is better than not trying."

Then he went into the house, retrieved the woman from the bottom of the pool, and took her down into the garden to a different place from the homeless guy. Not being terribly enthusiastic about this, he planned to bury her in a fairly shallow grave. Then, at the bottom of the hole, his shovel pried loose a corner of red cloth with a familiar red button on it.

Another Merrick memory floated by.

"Damn you and shut up."

He sighed, hauled the woman into the hole and covered her over with soil. It left an obvious grave mound. He was no good at this. Merrick would've been better at all of this shit. That man was better at everything, as well as ruthless.

Fuck him.

He should do something useful with the rest of his life, and he thought he knew what it should be. He would tidy up some loose ends.

Before he left.

CHAPTER TWELVE

Raffaela never returned, of course. She obeyed him.

Her decision both satisfied and frustrated? If frustration was the word for this bone-deep numbing ennui. He was tired of the world. What he'd had with her could not be surpassed. How could it be – an enthralling, obsessive, mind-blowing relationship with a siren?

She was correct. Siren was the better word. She had burrowed into his sexual psyche, his id, his soul, and left her mark there, and he hoped he'd left some sort of mark or memory on her heart and soul too.

Memories. Wolfgang spent many nights up on the pool level, sitting in the white lounger with a glass of whisky in hand, under the starry sky or the stormy sky, with the rest of the bottle at his feet or cuddled to his side like a baby.

All that research? It had been an excuse toward the end. None of it had been leading him anywhere. He needed a whole team and years to get any answers – if any answers were possible? He suspected a mermaid simply could not change back into being a human, permanently.

He wrote a memoir, a sort of late diary of their weeks together. Every event he could recall was detailed. He did sketches of her, especially of her tail because of its uniqueness, and of her face because she compelled him. The scales on her tail would have made perfect jewelry and it seemed such a pity none of that had been left to him. Not one single scale.

He sketched all of her in black and white, and never could he do her justice.

He wrote obscure love letters to her in the pages, and only realized that he'd been subconsciously doing so when he reached the date she had left. The day he set her free.

His pen had risen from the page. This was so personal.

He was right too, about what he had told her.

If she returned now, he would chain her up and keep her. Properly, this time.

A freshly bloomed red rose waited for him to use it, cut from a garden shrub. One of Merrick's. The whole flower would not fit inside the book. He fumbled over the side of the lounge, searching for the memoir.

Petal by petal, he plucked them to place one every few pages, then he closed the book and dropped the thorny stem to the grass. A gust blew it, and it rolled onto the pavers until it toppled, stilled, thorns up, with spiky shadows formed by an overhead light.

He took another gulp of whisky, surprised the ice was melted. The sea was quiet tonight, barely murmuring as it swept in and out. Yesterday he thought he'd caught a glimpse of a mermaid, or mer-something – one could not exactly sex them from that far away, and he was done with leaving drones in the ocean. He did not want to know.

If it was her after all, fuck her.

He threw the square tumbler into the pool where it sank

immediately.

"Fuck everyone!"

The next morning he woke in the lounge, arm numb, head throbbing, with the morning sun creeping into the sky.

Did he go on writing in diaries? No. He tongued his inner cheek, his teeth. His mouth tasted of dead things. His breath would likely kill a dog at ten paces.

It was time. Been a month or more and lately something inside him had been niggling him. His conscience? He did not think he had one of those. Maybe he had just had enough.

Enough, yes.

His resignation from the Institute had been sent long ago. Since he'd made a point of pissing off everyone there, repeatedly, nobody contacted him anymore. Wallowing in his aloneness was what he had wanted. Saturate himself in sorrow. He had cried his heart out to the sea, some days.

Shameless. Stupid. No one had seen. No one cared.

He did not deserve one jot of anything from anyone.

Time.

Though he dreaded the task he had set himself that first day she'd gone. After all, this was the beginning of the end. He meant to walk into the fucking sea once he was done. That was going to be bad.

Digging in the garden though… pretty sure it would be worse.

CHAPTER THIRTEEN

He rose, walked toward the steps that led down into the house and felt lancing pain in one foot. Discovered the rose stem stuck to his sole. He laughed and enfolded the stem in his fist, crushing it to his skin. Blood seeped from his fingers.

Karma.

He jogged down the stairs, gulped some water from the kitchen faucet, picked up a notepad and pen, then set off for the garden shed to fetch the shovel. The rose stem, he left on the sofa. He might throw it away later. The pain of the thorns though… he might need that again.

Now.

How many had there been? Seven?

He'd never asked if they were all here. Merrick had not said, and he'd not asked, preferring to not know. Preferring to think maybe his lover had let them go.

He knew though. He knew. No excuses. What was the likelihood of Merrick doing that? Zero?

Funny how this paralleled what he'd done, except he had actually let Raffaela go.

No excuses.

None.

He'd been as bad as Merrick. Though he used to leave for work and come back to find them gone, he'd also seen where the garden had been touched on those days.

Digging them up, deciding who was who from the clothes and hair color, from what was left of them, burying them again, then making a notation on the map of his property, yes, it was difficult.

By the end of the day, he was done. Completely done.

After showering until the hot water ran out, he headed for the fridge. Something cold and very alcoholic was desired...

Sitting on the sofa with a glass of red this time, he leaned hands on his knees, cupping the glass.

Map done.

Names on it. Probable dates of... taking them. Check to all of it.

Where they'd been found by Merrick in the first place, he left blank for all but one that Merrick had let slip. The rest, he didn't know.

He went into the study, laid out the map and took a pic, then attached it to the pre-written email.

One more deep breath. His mind felt blank of anything, full of nothing. This was it.

After this he would go.

If the cops read it straight away, he'd have the sirens and the knock at the door in a few hours, tops. A swarm of them, then him handcuffed, taken to the station, interrogated.

None of that was happening.

He pressed the send button.

After picking up the book, he went out the door that led to the beach. He stripped until he was naked, though he kept the memoir in one hand as if it were a bible. In the shallows where the water tickled over his feet and ankles, he stopped and breathed deep, smelling everything, seeing the seagulls whirling above him, the light fluffy clouds.

It was the waves that had been calling him.

They had reminded him of his vow.

Come, the waves said again. *Come to us.*

He raised the book, the memoir he had so painstakingly written. He drew back his arm, and he hurled it toward the deep. Then he walked in and kept walking until he floated.

And found out drowning himself wasn't so simple. His mind somehow thought he shouldn't inhale water. He began to tread water.

A hand grabbed his ankle, and *yanked*.

He'd been lured.

Lack of oxygen made everything blur as he was towed, molested, made love to, and he connected the dots as he drowned. This was a Ravening.

But he saw a face he recognized.

* * * * *

The light spread, fired up his mind. Brought him out of the darkness.

Water tinkled past his ears. *Fish and tails.* A gooey circle of light above, radiating down. That was the sun. The distant flowing shadow of a school of small fish, or of large ones? His eyes could not tell. His brain was not functioning as it should.

Underwater. Yes. And I'm breathing.

Wolfgang looked down the length of his body and saw a tail, and it was his.

The sex had been violent, bloody, and likely cataclysmic as well as amnesia inducing, but he was almost certain the pretty lips on his had been hers.

Then he had blanked.

Could it have been Raffaela?

Nothing had happened for a very, long time. Or at least, when he finally came into being and regained consciousness, eons seemed to have passed.

Was he alone? Slowly he spun, turning, turning.

Maybe he had been dreaming?

Either way he was here, and the future was full of grand possibilities. What more could a marine biologist wish for than a chance to see the world of the sea, like this, with the love of his life by his side?

He would find her.

He was a merman – somehow he'd converted – and if he had to search the seas for a year he would find her and make her his again.

A swirl and flick of long fair hair caught his eye and he spun again.

There.

CHAPTER FOURTEEN

Raffaela zoomed in before Wolfgang could have seen her properly, swinging around his waist, his now very muscular waist. The transformation to merman required the growth of stronger-than-human muscle else they would never be able to swim.

She half-clawed, half-kissed her way up his naked torso all the way to his delicious mouth,

By then Wolfgang had recovered and he took her face in his hands to tongue-kiss her properly. A warm, deep kiss that absorbed her completely until frissons of desire cascaded down her spine, until they shifted and their tails changed into legs.

Arousal had forced them both into human form. Their bodies drifted in the currents. Small fish dodged past, zipping around them. An immense, silvery school of sardines flooded by, shielding them from their surroundings.

Abruptly, his mouth opened wider and he tensed against her. There was a shove forward, then another pair of hands slipped about Wolfgang, over her arms. Big, male hands.

Merrick eyed her from over Wolfgang's shoulder, his jagged line of teeth converting to human type in seconds.

"Will I fuck your ass or hers, Wolfgang?"

His words had sounded like a purr, quite an achievement underwater.

She smiled and spoke, "Here is my surprise gift for you, my love." Her lips breathed on and brushed over Wolfgang's as the three of them pirouetted in the water, spiraling lower.

The ocean here was miles deep.

"Your Merrick survived also. This is how I knew what to do to make you one of us. The more prolonged and intense the lovemaking, the greater the love, the surer the result. We two are now three."

It shocked her to hear Wolfgang's first somber words to Merrick, "Do not ever hurt her, or I will feed you to a fucking shark."

Merrick laughed and kissed his back. "You know I would never do anything like that." He winked at her. "Thinks he owns you, huh? Wait until I tell him how many ways I've had you while he's been sleeping."

It was true. And somewhat blushworthy. The newly made merman was a lover to rival Wolfgang.

"The fuck you wouldn't." A threat again? Though the sigh that came from Wolfgang and the higher pitch of his words alerted her to Merrick doing something dirty to him.

She kicked her legs – even without a tail, negotiating the sea was easy. If he was screwing Wolfgang from behind, she wanted to watch this…

And also volunteer to be the filling in a sandwich made by their bodies.

The future was looking wonderful, and definitely not lonely.

Then Merrick grabbed her and dragged her into the

middle. "Come here, my mermaid fucktoy."

The sandwich was happening sooner than she'd imagined.

Wolfgang took little prompting, or none. His hot mouth descended on hers, his tongue swiping deep into her mouth, playing her, taunting her as he held her breast as if it were essential to life. She uttered tiny shocked noises at his shifting grip, at the twisting of her nipple and the crueler kissing. While Merrick... Merrick enthusiastically explored her back all the way down to her ass with hands and mouth. Then he reversed his journey, biting and kissing from her inner thighs to shoulders.

Some were large, shudder-inducing, bites of possession.

If the ocean was wet, she was far wetter.

Fingers slipped inside her, fucking her.

Still kissed, still held, then opened wider, with her legs spread by knees and hands, she whimpered, turning, writhing.

They swathed her in lust, thrust bare cocks at her ass or slid them along her slit. Her legs wrapped over Wolfgang and about his waist, she clutched him to her.

Until...

His hand clutched about her throat then Merrick impaled her at the rear, the head of his cock popping in, making her hold her breath, her heart thudding at the abrupt and somewhat painful intrusion.

He speared further, growling nonsensical curses, sucking his cock out, thrusting in, firmer, deeper. Wolfgang laughed into her neck, then leaned back. His eyes, she glimpsed those through the whirl of her hair while he stared at her face, probed at her pussy with his cock, and pushed at her.

In...

Both of them. The double penetration was mind-rending for the first few seconds.

She bowed her back, shut her eyes.

Someone latched onto her breast. And sucked at her.

With both of them kissing her, biting her, pistoning in, and with their hands on her *everywhere,* up and down became irrelevant.

Hurled into her first climax, she wrenched at someone's back with her nails, cutting into skin.

The taste of mer-blood entered the sea.

Sharks would not dare interrupt this wild, ecstatic embrace. They were not prey.

Enfolded again, murmured to, loved, stirred to new passion, she sighed in their grasp, groaned at the licking of her intimate places – such devotion in the use of warm tongues and mouths – at the delirious climb into fresh arousal.

She found a man and kissed down him, bit his thighs, only to be fucked by whoever was at her ass – they were slow, yet rough and forceful, and it was glorious.

The sea surged, caressing them all, and likely murmuring dirty words in her partner's ears.

Wolfgang and Merrick were inventive, and every hole on all of them seemed to be candidates to be fucked. She licked her way up and down cocks that were plunging into someone's ass or mouth, had hands wrapped in her hair or clawed at her butt while they made her do things she'd never thought to do.

The two of them managed to be inside her pussy for a sliver of time – it was the only time she blurted out a *no*.

And the sea washed them clean and slurred more filthy suggestions whenever calm befell them, then the passion would rise and rise, as inevitable as the tide. They were each enamored of the others' bodies, tasting, licking, tongues and cocks inserting, bodies bucking.

Upside-down was likely how they were oriented when yet again, both of her males speared inside her in unison.

Her hair twined about her like seaweed, blinding her.

Someone took her wrists, trapping them, fisting her hand about a cock. She jerked someone off, compelled to, as another fucked her mouth.

Leaked come streamed past, tracing their slow downward path.

Still they did not halt in their obsession with fucking her or each other. Not yet. The mindless abandon of a near-Ravening seemed to have taken them all past what was normal, sane, or stoppable.

They swapped places, over and over, circling her with wet, voracious kisses, nibbling her breasts, her belly, kissing each other, with their strong male muscles flexing. Biceps bulged, wrapped about each other's necks. Captivated, she watched them kiss until they hauled her back into the circle.

Merrick engulfed her nipple with heated mouth then fingered her below. Fingers in each hole.

"Ass and cunt," he assured her, smiling at her expression, pumping in and out. He seemed fascinated. She did not think she could come again, but...

With her thigh muscles trembling with fatigue, she watched him climb down her to eat her out with that determined tongue. When she squealed at the sensitive places he found, he held her hips to keep her against him, then... then Wolfgang moved in to screw him from behind.

The weird hum that came from Merrick then, with his lips glued to her clit. His tongue flattened, halted in place, seemed to become a part of her, then he licked. One long swipe, and he kept licking, sucking. A grunt as Wolfgang slapped in, behind him.

"Oh. Oh fuck. Fff..." She grabbed at Merrick's hair,

undulating.

Insatiable. The orgasms were relentless, and sometimes painful, as relentless as her men, her mermen.

Their leisurely spiral to the mile-deep bottom became a chaotic swirl.

It ended with them spinning through the last fathoms, with a cock in her mouth while the other one pounded at her, driving in then stopping deep, before he slammed in again, his cock feeling so large inside her pussy she thought she might burst.

Her cries were lost to the deep. Their violent lovemaking muddied the bottom with flying sand as they reached it.

Spent. Finally, peace came to them.

She lay entwined with her ear to Wolfgang's neck just below his ear. Arms around her, legs around her.

The ocean currents surged, pushed them.

Merrick was tangled about her limbs but up the other way, drifting and swaying, while he cradled against her legs.

"Thank you," she whispered to Wolfgang.

"Hmmm." He turned to press his lips to her nose, then to cup her face with his hand. "I have to say something. A confession, I suppose."

"Yes?" His pretty brown eyes regarded her from an eyelash away and she smiled. "Whatever you say, I am happy. If Merrick had not found me, I would never have known what to do. He helped me. He helped me figure out how to make you into this, one of my kind."

"I'm sure he did, but…"

"Yes?"

"The bad things I did, it was with Merrick. We killed girls, fucked them silly after we caught them. Fucked them for days, sometimes, used everything in that room you saw, and more. Then … Merrick killed them, buried them. I dug them up before I walked into the sea and sent an email to the cops so they know." He grimaced as if tasting something awful. "I'm a bad man. The fingers with the flesh falling off… some were mostly bones. Some…"

"Shhh." She placed her finger across his mouth. "You cannot comprehend the madness of this worry of yours. When your Ravening comes you will understand."

His frown deepened into a ravine between his eyebrows. He was amusing, cute.

"Oh, Wolfgang, my wonderful lover… I have killed a thousand humans, and together we will kill a thousand more. It is what we do. You and him? You are amateurs."

Then she smiled with her mermaid teeth. "This is why these are sharp. We are predators. Invisible, unseen, unstoppable when we want to be."

"Monsters." His eyes were wide.

"*Mmm.* That too. Now rest, my love. When you are ready, I will show you my world."

Then she pressed his eyes closed with kisses, making him sigh, and she snuggled in against his chest. Once upon a time, she had wanted to kill herself but not anymore, not when she had these two. Loneliness had been banished.

The ocean gently rocked them, making their beautiful tails move in the currents, as if it approved of these three precious beings, these pretty, pretty killers.